When romance author Delu Morris is troubled with unexplained panic attacks, she seeks help from a doctor who's researching dream-therapy. He explains that he'll accompany her into her dreams to revisit her memories and to try to uncover if an event from her past is causing her trouble now.

His grad assistant is a handsome Scotsman who wears a kilt the first time he meets her. She's intrigued, but they remain at arms' distance while he's a part of her therapy team. When she discovers that only he can make the machine work, he confesses that he's the 7th son of a 7th son, and the Unseelie are using him for some unknown reason. When he touches the controls, he pushes a *wee bit o' magic* into the machine to make it work.

Will they discover together what her long-lost memory is? Or will the guilty person manage to keep her from that discovery — for good?

Gaelic Magic
Copyright © 2022 Fiona McGier
ISBN: 978-1-4874-3735-0
Cover art by Martine Jardin

Published by eXtasy Books Inc

Look for us online at:
www.eXtasybooks.com

Gaelic Magic

By

Fiona McGier

DEDICATION

Note: Me late faither was from Glesca, crossing the pond when he was 21, fresh out of the British army. I've never even wanted to read, let alone write a Highlander romance, because the accent says **Hello, Dad** *to me. But this story came to me in a dream — as many of my book plots have. And when I get inspired by dreams, I always end up writing those stories. I've tried to be true to me faither's accent — so I've made the hero also be from Glasgow, so their accents are the same.*

CHAPTER ONE

The line was long, and the people, some of whom had been waiting for hours, were getting restless.

"What's taking so long? I've been here for over two hours! She's up there signing books, right?"

The woman in front of the complainer was taller. "Yes, she's up there. But people are making conversation with her, instead of just having her sign the book. And some have brought older books too, so she's signing more than one for lots of them."

"That's totally not fair! It said it right in the rules on-line that she would only sign her newest book, and only if you bought it here."

A professional-looking woman strode purposefully along past the line of readers.

Recognizing her, the taller woman addressed her. "Hey, you work here, right?"

The woman nodded. "Yes, I'm the manager. What can I do for you?"

"It looks like some of the people up there are having Ms. Morris sign more than one book. Your directions on-line clearly stated that she would only sign one book per reader."

The woman frowned as she looked up toward the front of the line. "That's what I was afraid of. She's too nice. One of my employees was up there to be sure that didn't happen, but she just went on break. I'll soon put a stop to that. So sorry for the inconvenience." With a quick nod to those in line, she turned and walked quickly up to the front of the line.

1

"What's she doing?" The shorter reader was still not able to see anything.

"She's leaning over talking to Ms. Morris. Now she's talking to the person who has multiple books lined up for signatures. I really like the manager. She knows when to take charge of a situation, and she doesn't take any crap from anyone."

"Hurray!" Many of the others in line nodded when the line started to slowly move again.

With the manager right behind her, the author resumed signing only one book per reader, and the two who had been so impatient soon had their chance to chat briefly with the author as she signed their books. Both graced the manager with huge smiles as they walked away, happy with their new treasure.

Naomi stood up to stretch her tired muscles. The line was much shorter now, but she'd been signing books for so many hours that her hand was cramping. And her cheeks felt the strain of smiling non-stop. "Just give me a minute, okay?" She implored the older woman who was next in line.

She nodded, smiling. "Anything for you, Ms. Morris. I'm a huge fan of your books! When my husband passed away two years ago, they were the only thing to keep me from total depression. There will never be another man to replace my Hugh. But your heroes at least remind me that there are men like them around . . . even if just in books."

Naomi nodded with a grin. "I'm glad that you had a good man. I still haven't met *the one* yet. I'm getting tired of warts on my lips from all of the frogs I keep kissing, trying to find Prince Charming." She smiled as she sat back down and picked up the pen again.

"Just you keep on looking, honey," the reader replied. "A

gorgeous woman like you, with such a romantic soul, deserves the very best kind of man. One who will appreciate you for the jewel you are."

"Do you know my mother? Or my grandmother? That's what they keep telling me. To whom should I dedicate this book?"

"My name is Elaine."

Naomi spoke out loud as she wrote. "To Elaine, who had the good fortune to have had Hugh as her husband. May she find another good man for the second half of her life. Love, Delu Morris."

"Oh, thank you, Ms. Morris! And I'll pray for you to find the man you're looking for . . . maybe very soon."

Naomi's eyes sparkled as she nodded, then turned to the next person in line.

Another couple of hours had passed, and the line was much shorter, but there were still people waiting, books in hand. Suddenly a man's loud voice cut through the ambient noise from the crowded store. He was haranguing a woman at the back of the line.

"How long do you expect me to wait around with my thumb up my ass? You know I hate waiting around. And I especially hate bookstores."

"Go out and have another smoke, Jerry." The woman he was talking to shifted nervously around from one foot to the other. "This is the shortest the line has been all day."

"I know. You've been making me walk past this damn store for hours. If you're not done and outside by the time I finish another smoke, I'm leaving and you can have that author give you a ride home. Or you can walk."

"You can't do that! It's my car."

"Just watch me, bitch."

She grabbed the man's arm to detain him, and his temper

appeared to snap. His hand drew up as if he was going to slap her.

Naomi felt hot. Her heart was pounding as blood rushed quickly through her veins. The hand holding the pen began to shake, and she realized, to her horror, that she was sliding into a panic attack.

"What's wrong?" The reader who was next in line asked.

The manager peered into her face. "Are you all right, Ms. Morris?"

Naomi shook her head weakly. "No. I think I need to leave . . .right now." She stood up and felt the room move as she held onto the table to stop herself from swaying.

The manager spoke into a tiny transmitter clipped to her sweater. A minute later, a security guard appeared near the arguing couple. He tapped the man on the shoulder. The outraged man whirled around, then pulled back his fist again and took a swing at the guard. The guard earned his salary by managing to stop the blow. He also neutralized the threat by grabbing the man's other arm and twisting it behind him so he could walk him toward the door.

The woman who had been in line followed them, words spilling out of her. "Don't hurt him. It's not his fault. It's mine. He just gets antsy when he's got to wait in line. I won't press any charges against him." Her voice trailed off as they walked out through the front door.

Naomi was still shaking when the manager looked her way again, her nerves not done reacting to what had set off her anxiety alarms. "I think you've signed enough books today, Ms. Morris. Go splash some cool water on your face. It will help you feel better." Naomi staggered toward the back of the store, where the restrooms were, and heard the manager address the unhappy customers still in line.

"We have some pre-signed books from Ms. Morris. You can exchange the one you picked up on the way in the store for one of them. And to help alleviate your disappointment at not getting it personalized, you'll receive a coupon good for fifteen percent off of your next purchase, either on-line or in the store."

Naomi was panting—not from exertion, but from anxiety—when she finally made it to the bathroom. She fell into a stall, locked the door, and sat down, fully clothed, taking deep breaths, trying to get her nerves back under control. Finally, her heartbeat slowed enough for the knot of tension to ease in her chest, and she was able to draw in a full breath. After a few minutes of normal breathing, she opened the stall and went over to run the water in the sink until it got cold. She cupped her hands under the flow and lowered her face to splash some of it onto her flushed skin. She leaned closer to the mirror, staring into her own eyes.

What the hell is wrong with me? I never used to have panic attacks before. But lately I've had a few dreams that made me wake up in a sweat, breathing so hard it was like I was running a marathon. I've always been able to remember my dreams before – that's how I've gotten some of my best story ideas. But when I wake up shaking, I can never remember anything except an overwhelming feeling of fear.

And now it's happened a few times when I was awake, too. I don't put much stock into therapy, but I think I need to find someone to help me figure out what's going on in my head. Am I going crazy? Do I need to be medicated? I sure hope not. That might interfere with my creativity. But either way, I've got to figure this out so it doesn't keep happening.

By the time the manager came back to check on her, Naomi was pulling on her jacket in the break room. She whirled around when the door opened, expecting a threat.

"It's only me, my dear. I wanted to be sure you were all right."

Naomi nodded slowly. "Thanks. And thanks for finding a way to get me away from the line of readers. I'm sorry to disappoint them, but it's been a really long day for me."

The manager smiled, speaking gently. "You probably haven't eaten anything for hours. Do you want me to bring you anything from the coffee bar?"

"No. I think I'll head on home. I need a hot cup of tea and a warm blanket."

"Promise you'll eat something, too?"

Naomi's lips turned up. "Yes, *Mom*. I promise. Then maybe I'll make it an early night. I think I've been working too hard lately."

Satisfied that she had a plan, she walked out of the break room and made her way out of the store via the employee exit in the back.

As soon as she got back to her apartment, she started water for her tea and went on-line to look up local therapists in or close to her hometown of Blacksburg, Virginia.

Chapter Two

Naomi looked around with interest at her surroundings as she walked into the inner sanctum of the famous dream-therapist who was late for his appointment. There were three doors in the room. She had entered through one of them. She wondered what the other two doors led to. She didn't have long to wait. One of the doors swung open, and a tall, bald man with a dark gray mustache and goatee walked through it, smiling broadly as she rose to introduce herself.

"You must be Delu Morris. While I must confess that I haven't read any of your books, I did download one onto my e-reader last night. From what little I read, it's no wonder that you're such a successful author. And my secretary tells me she owns all of your books."

She smiled back at the affable older man. "Thanks. And you must be Doctor Banning. You come highly recommended by a close friend. I've read about your work, and I'm honored to meet you, sir."

He took her hand in a brief shake before gesturing toward the chair she'd perched on before he entered the room. "Please don't call me *sir*," he began with a grimace. "It's bad enough to be getting old, but to have a beautiful young woman call me that makes me feel like I have one foot in the grave and the other on a banana peel. My full name is Doctor Cedric Alan Banning. I'd prefer if you call me Doctor Alan."

He sat down on a chair that faced hers, both of them on the same side of his over-sized desk that dominated the office.

"All right, Doctor Alan. Actually, Delu Morris is my pen

name. My real name is—"

"Naomi Delu Morrison," he read from the file that he had carried into the office with him. "You're twenty-eight years old. Your mother is Marie Gaubert Morrison, a Black woman who met John Morrison, your white father, when they attended the same college. He's a self-made man who invested early in new technologies, particularly in the farming industry, making quite a name for himself, as well as a comfortable life for his family. You grew up in Richmond, attending all the finest private schools that money could buy. You spent your summers on an estate near Lynchburg, owned by the Reynolds family, where your maternal grandmother lives in an old servant's cottage and works as their cook."

Naomi frowned. "She prefers to be called their *chef*."

The doctor smiled affably. "Ah. I was merely reading from the information your agent provided. But I need to know who you are and why you're here, in your own words. Perhaps you can explain things better?"

"You seem to think you already know who I am, so let's just leave it at that. As to why I'm here, a long-time friend of the family suggested that I try out your new experimental therapy. I honestly didn't think that anyone else outside of my immediate family knew that I've been having weird dreams lately, along with panic attacks. I figured it was just something I'd get over sooner or later. But I guess Dad golfed with the friend recently and told him about me. He said that your experimental *dream-therapy* as he called it, was proving helpful to other people, so I should give it a try."

Dr. Banning leaned forward. "And what do you expect my therapy process to accomplish for you?"

Naomi shrugged. "I don't know. Maybe figure out what's causing me to have the same anxiety dreams repeatedly? Maybe get them to stop? And stop me from having panic attacks in public. Hopefully, without medication that might dampen my creativity."

"Are you experiencing distress over anything in your life right now?"

She shook her head. "Other than the ordinary panic of wondering whether or not I will ever be able to write another book? Or if readers will get tired of my scribbling and rush to join the throng praising the next big thing?" Naomi waved both hands in the air. She felt a burst of pleasure as she admired the nails she had to keep short for typing, but that she paid her manicurist to decorate. "Other than that? Nah. Same old, same old. Just the usual author worries."

"I see. Let's go into the next room, and I can show you what my therapy involves. That way you can make an informed decision as to whether or not you want to begin twice-weekly visits to try to track down what's bothering you."

They both got up. Naomi followed the doctor to the third door she'd observed. He unlocked it, then motioned for her to precede him into the room. The light turned on automatically as she entered. The room was crowded with electronics—wires protruded from the equipment. There were two reclining chairs placed closely together, facing in opposite directions. She approached them, then turned to look at the man inquisitively.

"Are these the chairs we'll be sitting in while we're in my dreams?"

Dr. Banning smiled and walked to a large, imposing box and patted it. "Yes, my dear. You'll sit in one chair, reclining to a comfortable position. And I will do the same in the other chair. We'll both be hooked up to this machine, which will allow me to enter your dreams with you."

Her eyebrows rose. "You go into someone's head? Into their dreams? How?"

He gestured to the wires that were draped over the ends of both chairs. The other ends of the wires were neatly arranged on the table that was in between the chairs. "You will find that out tomorrow, presuming you want to engage my services."

She made a face and felt her anxiety rise. Dr. Alan must have noticed it. "You're not feeling anxiety about the procedure itself, are you, Ms. Morrison?"

She shook her head slowly. "No. And I guess you should call me by my first name. After all, if you're going to be in my head with me, it seems silly to be so formal."

He nodded. "Then you wish to continue? Good."

"Is there any pain with your technique? I mean, should I take anything before I get here?"

"No. There's no pain. In fact, many patients report feeling well-rested after a session of guided-active-dreaming. The only negative that's been mentioned is that people are not used to having other voices in their head, so that can be distressing at first until they get used to it."

Naomi laughed heartily.

The man waited for her to stop. "What's so funny?"

"Those other people must not be authors."

"To date, I've not treated any other author. You will be my first. Why?"

She shook her head, smiling. "There are often *other people* talking in my head. I doubt I'll even notice one more voice. That's part of why I write books, Dr. Alan. Once the book is done, that set of characters stops talking to me. But it doesn't take long before another set starts insisting that I tell their story next."

He studied her face. "What you're describing sounds quite similar to schizophrenia."

She nodded. "Yeah. But when I told my parents that's how I write, they sent me to a couple of different analysts. They concluded that I'm functioning just fine in my daily life by any measure. All the voices do is tell me stories. None of them have encouraged me to attack anyone or cause harm in any way. Actually, I've always thought of them as my best friends. When you're brought up like I was, you can't ever be sure who your friends really are. If the kids who tell you they like you just want to ride your ponies, or play with your toys. Or date your cute brothers. But the voices in my head are always there for me."

"I see." He sounded unconvinced.

She smiled at him. "It's okay. I doubt they'll want anything to do with you. They only talk to me. But then, I've never had anyone else in my head with me before. This should be interesting, even if you can't help me find out what's causing my anxiety dreams and panic attacks."

He nodded. "It should be interesting indeed."

"So I'll make an appointment with your secretary on my way out, then?"

"Yes. Tell her to schedule you for this Friday morning.

And you will be coming here twice-weekly for at least three additional weeks. That should give us an idea of how well you respond to my therapy and whether the solution will be easily found. We can always schedule more visits if we need them."

"Okay. See you on Friday, Dr. Alan."

"Oh, and one more thing, Ms. Morris. Be sure to wear comfortable clothing, since you'll be primarily sleeping here."

Her eyebrows rose. "Uh, okay. I will."

He walked with her out to the room she had seen first, then sat on the chair behind the desk as he watched her walk towards the door. He allowed himself a brief introspection on his new client.

What a great ass that woman has! Her hips sway so seductively as she walks — like poetry in motion. Yes, my dear. I'm looking forward to being inside of you for many weeks to come.

CHAPTER THREE

On Friday morning, Naomi spent some time wondering just what she would be comfortable sleeping in with the doctor in the room. *I got the impression that he's kind of a dirty old man. Not from anything he actually said, but just a vibe I felt from him. So I don't want to dress to be sexy at all. Maybe I'll just wear a pair of jeans and a t-shirt, with my soft and comfy flannel shirt over it.*

Satisfied that she had a good plan, she got dressed. She didn't even apply any make-up, since all she was going to be doing was sleeping. And having woken up with raccoon-eyes in the past, she knew that mascara was not a good idea for sleepwear. She ate a quick breakfast of yogurt with fruit and walnuts in it, then only had one cup of coffee. She took it with her to finish along the way as she drove to her ten o'clock appointment. She was in the office talking to the secretary by nine-forty-five.

"I love your books, Ms. Morris. If I bring some of them in next week, will you sign them for me? I've only got your newest one with me now since I eat my lunch at my desk, and I read while I eat."

"I'd be glad to sign that one for you now. Your name is Margaret, right? And bring as many as you want for next week. I'm going to be coming here for at least the next few weeks, so we have plenty of time for me to sign your books."

"I usually go by Maggie, so please use that when you sign."

As she was signing the book for the secretary, Naomi asked in a casual tone, "When I'm with the doctor, will there be anyone else in the room?"

The secretary nodded. "Oh, yes. There needs to be someone in there to run the equipment while the doctor is in your memories with you. "

"Is it a nurse?"

"Oh no, Ms. Morris. It's a grad student who's doing his internship. His name is Will."

The intercom buzzed, and the secretary smiled as she took her signed book back from Naomi. She held it closely to her bosom, as if it was a precious heirloom. "You can go in now, Ms. Morris."

Naomi grinned. "Please, you're going to be seeing me twice every week. And since you've read my books, in a way, you've actually already been in my head. Call me Naomi. It's my real name, you know. Delu is my middle name, as well as my pen name."

The secretary smiled shyly. "Okay . . . Naomi."

As she entered the office, the first thing that Naomi noticed was that both of the doors were already open. Since the doctor wasn't in his office, she went over to peer into the next room. Her eyebrows rose in surprise, and a smile spread across her lips.

The young man who was working on some equipment looked up to grin at her.

"Yer Ms. Morris, right? The author? Ah'm Will. The doctor will be here in 'alf a tick. Please come in and have a seat while Ah get things set up."

Naomi walked slowly over to the nearest reclining chair and perched on it. "Do you always wear a kilt, mister—"

He smiled, nodding.

Lordy, look at those bright blue eyes! They're so light they're almost clear. His hair is almost black—so striking with that pale skin. He looks like what I've always imagined my Duncan to look like.

"Nae always, but often. It's what Ah'm most comfortable in. Ah hope me accent isnae too thick for ye to understand me.

14

Muh name is William Hamilton, but ye can call me Will. Ah'm here doin' muh grad work through Virginia Tech. It's an honor to meet a real author. Especially one that ma maither and sister have read."

She smiled at him. "Hello, Will. My real name is Naomi Delu Morrison. You can call me Naomi. Are you going to be in my dreams also?"

He shook his head. "That's no muh place. Ah'll be here, making sure that all o' the connections stay live to keep Dr. Banning in yer heed."

"Well, now, that's a real shame. There's someone who lives in my head who I'd like you to meet. You look very much like one of my heroes."

He snorted, a short bark of laughter that he tried to cover up with a cough. "Aye, that'd be your Laird Duncan MacLeod? Ma maither said ye didnae gi'e him the proper accent. But then, yer from the colonies. You folks dinnae ken that much about regional differences in the accents from back home."

Her eyebrows rose. "You sound just like he does, when he talks in my head."

"Aye, that's the point. The MacLeods are from the north, so they have a very different accent. The Hamiltons are from the south—near Glesga. Actually, where Ah'm from, ye can almost tell what side of the street someone grew up on based on how they speak. Maybe to you it sounds the same. But to mah ear, it's very distinctive."

At that moment, the doctor strode into the room. "Ah, you're here. I see you've met my assistant. Has he explained anything to you?"

Naomi shook her head. "No, we were discussing why the accent that I've given to my Scottish hero is all wrong for where his clan is from. I wonder if that affects my sales in the UK?"

"Ah dinnae think so, lassie. Ah telt ye, ma maither and sister were willing to overlook sich minor details. Ah would think other readers would as well."

The doctor gave a stern look to his assistant. "Will, can you tone it down a bit, so I can understand you better? Now let's get down to business, shall we?"

The harsh tone surprised Naomi and she frowned. *Is he jealous that I was talking to his assistant? Dude, you're old enough to be my dad, at least — maybe even my grandfather. Chill out!* Aloud, she asked him, "Do you want me to lie back now?"

"No, Naomi. First, I need to explain the process to you so you'll know what's going to happen." He waved toward the large piece of unfamiliar-looking technology that Will was fiddling with. "My grad student is getting all of the wires hooked up to the machine that will provide me access to your memories and dreams. Once he's done, then I'll ask you to lie back and get comfortable. At that point, I'll hold a bottle under your nose and ask you to breathe deeply. It's an organic herbal extract that will relax your body and your mind.

"Then I'll use some minor hypnosis to induce a sleep-like condition. Once you're in a relaxed state, my assistant will apply the wires to your forehead and your temples. I will also apply the same wires in the same places on my head, and he'll switch the machine on. At that point, you might feel strange. Like I said, most patients are surprised to have another person speaking in their minds."

She smiled. "And as I told you, that's happened to me almost every single day of my life. My characters are always speaking in my head, telling me their stories. That's why I need quiet to write . . . so I can hear their words. I don't think I'll mind having one more voice in my head."

He turned to Will. "Ready?"

Will nodded. "Aye, sir. Whenever you are."

The doctor nodded to her. "Naomi, please make yourself comfortable."

She sat more fully on the chair and leaned back. She looked expectantly at the doctor.

"Relax."

She kicked off her shoes, rustling her arms and legs until they felt like they were in a comfortable position. The minute she stopped moving, the doctor waved a bottle under her nose and she inhaled deeply.

"Now close your eyes, please, Naomi."

With her eyes closed, she wasn't sure who was applying the pads to her forehead and her temples, but when she inhaled again, she didn't smell the doctor's after-shave or the oil from the bottle—but a light cedar smell that must have come from the Scottish grad student. A smile crept across her lips.

"That's right. Relax. Listen to the sound of my voice, and repeat the mantra with me. *Oh-mah. Oh-mah. Oh-mah.*"

Naomi felt her body relax as she murmured the sounds and her mind began to drift along on a current of the repeated syllables. Without even realizing what was happening, she was soon asleep.

"She's under, Will. Please help me hook myself into the machine so we can proceed."

Will stepped forward, and within a few minutes, the doctor had pads with wires running out of them stuck onto his head in the same places they were on Naomi. He was on the other reclining chair, and he leaned back, first inhaling the herbal scents, then repeating the sounds a few times as he closed his eyes.

Will placed both of his hands on the control knobs for the machine, and the therapy began.

Naomi looked around in surprise. She was lying in bed in her apartment, and her alarm was going off. She jumped when a voice spoke very close to her ear.

"Relax, Naomi. It's only me, Doctor Alan. Since this is our first time, I only want to ensure that our connection is strong enough for us to journey together into your memories. So, we're starting slowly with your memories from this morning."

Alarmed at his nearness, she turned her head to see that he wasn't actually in bed with her — he was standing next to her bed. He must have lowered his head down in order to speak into her ear.

"Um, okay. What happens now?"

"What do you usually do when you get up?"

"Uh, I get up to use the bathroom."

"Go ahead. I'll wait."

After doing her business, she walked back into her bedroom to see him standing by her window.

He nodded to her. "Then what do you do?"

"I start my coffeemaker, then I get dressed."

"No shower?"

"Uh, no. I like to shower before I go to sleep at night."

"I see. All right, do all of your morning things."

"You're not coming with me into the bathroom, right? I mean, I know you need to get to know me very closely, but I draw the line at you watching me get dressed."

There was a loud sigh. "If you feel that way, then yes, I'll wait here while you get dressed."

She knew that morning she'd spent some time in her bra and panties, trying to figure out what to wear. But there was no way she was going to stand around half-nude in front of the doctor who gave off pervy vibes. Plus, she already knew what she'd chosen to wear, so she brought her clothing with her into the bathroom and dressed in record time. When she opened the door, the doctor was standing in the same position.

He smiled. "Now what? Without talking to me, show me what you did this morning."

Since she was dressed, she felt infinitely safer, so she stopped talking to him and reenacted her morning movements. She got her breakfast out, ate it, made her coffee, and only drank part of it, then she walked out of her condo, closing the door behind her.

Once again, the doctor leaned very close to her from behind, inhaling briefly before he spoke to her gently. "Now what?"

"Do you have to stand so close to me all the time?"

"Actually, yes. Remember, Naomi, we're getting ready to delve deeper into your memories. Most of the time, we won't be speaking to each other directly. I'll merely be watching as you interact with other people from your past. I'll see what you see. I'll experience your feelings, to some extent. You are the one in control here. I'm just an observer."

"Then I'm not going to talk to you anymore."

He nodded. "Very good."

He followed her down the stairs to her car and slipped into the passenger seat as she started it up. She tried not to be self-conscious as she drove to his office. He shadowed her after that, watching silently as she chatted with his secretary. Then he followed her into the lab, where she interacted with his grad student. She was sure she felt displeasure radiating from the good doctor as she spoke with Will.

Abruptly, the connection was broken and she woke up.

She took a deep breath, then let out a sigh.

"No, don't try to sit up too quickly," the doctor said from the chair next to her head. "It can give you a disoriented feeling, waking up from shared dreaming."

"I think I'm okay." She sat up and nodded her head, front and back, then side-to-side.

"No odd feelings? No dizziness?"

She shook her head. "Nope."

"Very good. Then I'll see you again next Tuesday. And the Friday after that."

"How long do you think it will take?"

He shrugged. "That depends on how deeply buried the issue or event is that's causing you to feel anxiety and panic attacks. I suspect you have what we call *Dissociative Amnesia*. It's when a memory is so painful that it overwhelms the central nervous system and forces you to split off that memory from your conscious awareness. It's a common symptom of Post-Traumatic Stress Syndrome."

"But I've never been in that kind of stressful situation."

The doctor stared at her intently. "Not that you can remember."

Her eyes widened as she realized the full extent of what the doctor was insinuating. She spoke in a shaky voice. "So how long does this usually take?"

He shrugged. "Every case is different. I'd guess it will be for at least three weeks."

"All right. I'll make a few appointments with Maggie on the way out." She got up, ignoring the solicitous hand the doctor proffered to help her stand. "I'm fine. See you next week."

She shoved her feet into her sandals and smiled at both men before walking out the door, closing it behind her.

The older man turned to Will. "Please remember to keep your accent under control around our patients, Will. It can get so thick I can't understand what you're saying."

Will looked up from the pads on the wires that he was cleaning. "Aye, doctor. Ah'll be careful. It's just that since she's written books about Highlanders, Ah thought she'd be amused to hear what a real Scotsman sounds like."

Cedric gave him a sharp look. "Have you read any of her books?"

Will shook his head. "Nae me, but ma maither and sister have."

"Well, if you do, remember that the books are fiction, not real life. And that Ms. Morrison is a patient of ours. So there is no possibility of a romantic entanglement between you. I would have to report you to your mentoring professor."

Will's eyebrows rose. "Ach aye. Ah know that, Doctor Banning."

The doctor turned and walked through the side door to go into his private office.

As he finished cleaning up the equipment, Will muttered to himself. "Ach, it's no *me* Ah'm worried aboot, ya letch. But you'll be keeping your hands to yoursel' while in her dreams. Ah'll make sure o' that. She's too young and beautiful for the likes of you."

CHAPTER FOUR

Naomi spent some time over the weekend trying to remember if there was anything in her past that might indicate why she was now prone to panic attacks. When nothing occurred to her, she decided to work with the doctor and his dream analysis for a while to see what he came up with.

So on Tuesday morning, she once again dressed for comfort and strolled into the reception area a few minutes earlier so she'd have time to sign a few books for the pleasant woman who was his secretary. "Good morning, Maggie. Did you remember to bring in your books for me to sign?"

The older woman blushed, nodding. "Yes, but I only brought in some of them. I don't want to monopolize your time or make you get writer's cramp from signing." She held up four books.

"Ah, I see you really like my *Spies in the Skies* series. You've got the most recent three of them."

Maggie nodded. "And I brought in the first book I ever read by you. It's the first Scottish Highlander book about Laird Duncan MacLeod. The cover model was so dreamy that I bought it on a whim, just because of him."

Naomi looked up from signing the other books, grinning. "You just made a rhyme. You're a poet, and you don't know it. Okay, hand it over."

"Be careful with it. I've read it so many times the pages are almost falling out."

Naomi smiled. "I'll see if I can get my publisher to send you a new copy. Avid fandom like yours deserves to be rewarded."

"Are you working on anything new now?"

She shook her head as she looked up. "Not really. These panic attacks I've been having are giving me writer's block, I think. I've got ideas floating around, but whenever I sit down at my laptop, unwelcome thoughts swirl around in my head. That's one of the reasons that I'm coming here for Doctor Alan's treatments. I'm hoping that once I find out what's causing me to feel so anxious, I'll be able to tap back into my creativity and get going on some new stuff for you to read."

There was a beep on the telephone console. Maggie smiled at Naomi. "He's ready for you now."

Naomi headed in through the doorway to the lab. Without thinking, she spoke to the assistant. "Will, I'm so disappointed that you're not in a kilt this week. I've been hoping that seeing you in one and talking to you would help inspire me to write another Laird Duncan MacLeod novel. Readers have been clamoring for one, but I've got some writer's block issues, what with these anxiety attacks and all."

Will smiled at her but said nothing.

The older man in the room nodded. "Yes, Naomi. I think your writing problems are probably related to your tension over the unaccustomed panic attacks you've been having recently."

As she sat down on the recliner that was her sleeping place, Naomi frowned, looking at the doctor. "So, you really have no idea how long I'll have to come to see you?"

He shook his head. "Not really. That depends on a lot of things. But most of all, on your age when whatever has resurfaced beneath your consciousness happened."

"Does it have to be an event? Can't it just be general discontent?"

"No. For panic attacks as severe as you've reported having, there must be a triggering event that's buried in your memories somewhere. The sooner we find it, the sooner you can get back to your writing career." He gave her a sly look. "And maybe you'll be inspired to write about a tall, dark, and handsome therapist in your next book."

Will snorted quietly. Because he was next to Naomi, applying the electrodes to her, she heard it. The doctor was checking his notes on the counter across the room. He didn't appear to have heard anything.

Naomi shared a secret smile with Will. *Lord! When he smiles, he's got dimples to die for! A tall red-blooded Scotsman with black hair, dimples, wears kilts, and has a sexy accent? I wonder what else about him might fit the qualifications of my perfect man. From what I've seen, his ass does look damn fine in those tight jeans. Yum!*

Will continued to connect the other ends of the electrodes to the machine as the doctor came over. "Today, I think we should explore some of your more recent memories."

"Do you mean like the last time?"

He shook his head. "No. That was just to get you used to the feeling of someone else being in your head with you. No, I want to explore any recent dealings you've had with men. Any arguments, in particular. You said that the couple arguing in line appeared to be what set you off when you were at your book signing."

"Yes, but it also might have been because I was exhausted from such a long day of signing books, and I hadn't eaten anything for hours."

"Never-the-less, the arguing is what precipitated your headache and your anxiety. So, I need to know, are you dating anyone now?"

Naomi shook her head.

"Have you dated anyone recently? Like maybe had a break-up?"

"Well, yes. I was dating this guy named Brian that I met through a mutual friend. He told her he wanted to meet me, so she had us both over to a party at her place. We hit it off and dated for a few months."

"When did your relationship end?"

"He wasn't the cause of the anxiety, if that's what you're thinking. I'd been having the panic attacks before I even met him."

"Yes, but it might be worth exploring to see if he exacerbated the situation. Maybe your break-up with him made things worse."

Naomi's lips turned up slightly. "Or maybe you're ascribing more importance to him than he deserves. It was only a few months."

"Humor me, Naomi."

"So do you have to tell me where we're going in my memories ahead of time? Is that how this whole thing works?"

"Sometimes. And other times, we'll be in one memory, then another one will present itself. That's the optimum occurrence, because usually that's the one we need to get at, but your conscious mind doesn't want to allow it."

"Okay, then we're going to start at the party when I met him?"

He nodded. "Then quickly breeze through your relationship to get to the end. I presume it was you who ended things?"

"Yeah, it was. I knew he wasn't right for me, even though he thought he was."

He looked up at Will. "Is she connected?"

Will nodded. "Aye, doctor. And yer wires are ready for you."

The doctor moved over to the machine, taking a few moments to appraise the connections Will had finished. "Looks good. I think we're ready to begin. Naomi, please lie back and concentrate on breathing deeply. Clear your mind of anything other than thinking about your relationship with Brian."

He held the container of soothing oil under her nose again

as she took deep breaths. "That's right. Breathe in for six counts, then out for six counts. In and out, slowly, deliberately. Feel the air moving in and out of your lungs. Go deeper into the feeling of relaxation."

Naomi wasn't aware of when the doctor went over to the chair that he sat on and reclined it. But his voice was further away from her when he spoke next.

"It's time for us to chant together, Naomi. Say it with me, please. *Oh-mah. Oh-mah. Oh-mah.*"

Naomi wasn't aware of her chanting ending because she was already in her memories.

She looked around and realized she was at the party that Ellie had thrown to celebrate Naomi's new book release. There were streamers in the same red and black colors that were on the book cover. It was summer, so everyone was in shorts and tank tops. Naomi had come in wearing a sundress. She looked down at her dress and smiled.

I look good in this color. Yellow and chartreuse are so vivid on my brown skin color. I'm glad this isn't a formal party. My feet are still killing me from having to wear heels for the opening day party at the big bookstore downtown yesterday.

"There you are! The star of the party! Naomi, come with me and meet some of the folks just dying to meet you! Some of them didn't even know that I have the famous author Delu Morris on speed dial on my phone! But we go way back, don't we, sweetie?"

Naomi grinned. "Yeah. Back to grade school when you teased me unmercifully about my 'fro, calling it retro-chic. I didn't know what you were talking about. But just to be sure, I punched you in case it was a bad thing."

Ellie giggled. "Then we both got dragged down to the principal's office. When she found out what I'd said that made you punch me, it was hard for her not to laugh. That's what she told my mom later. But we had to sit in the hall for so long waiting for her that by the time we got into her office, we were friends. And that was twenty years ago."

Naomi enjoyed herself, circulating around, meeting people she didn't know and reconnecting with Ellie's friends that she knew from previous parties. Suddenly the air near her was invaded by the smell of a spicy after-shave. She turned her head to see a blond man with a mustache staring at her.

"Can I help you? If you want a picture of me, buy one of my books. That way you can look at me all you want."

He grinned at her. "I was just basking in the glory of you, Ms. Morris. Ellie told me you'd be here, and I've been excited all week knowing I'd be able to meet you today."

"I see. And you are?"

"Brian Thompson. I'm a very distant cousin of Ellie's, from Omaha. My family has a place near here, so that's where I'm staying while I'm working on a book."

"Oh? You're a writer also?"

He nodded. "Yes. I write technical journals for nerds who want to know everything there is to know about the latest games my company produces. I also write the instructions for new players. Are you a gamer, Ms. Morris?"

She shook her head, smiling. "Um, no. I'm more of a book nerd, not a gaming nerd. When I'm not writing my own books, I'm usually reading someone else's. And please, call me Naomi."

He raised his eyebrows. "Not Delu?"

"No. That's my middle name. My real name is Naomi Delu Morrison. I shortened it to the pen name of Delu Morris."

"Doesn't Naomi mean beautiful?"

She grinned at him. "Why yes, it can be that. It can also mean pleasant. And Delu means first girl born after three boys. But you obviously already knew my real name because you looked up the meaning of it. Right?"

"Guilty as charge, ma'am. I wanted to have a way to give you a compliment immediately. Then I can be suave and debonair and monopolize you for the rest of the party. Is that all right with you?"

"Maybe. I reserve judgment until I see just how suave you can be."

27

"Agreed."

Her memories jumped ahead to give a glimpse of the early dates she had with Brian. They didn't have sex until they'd been dating for a few weeks. When they did, it was a sophisticated evening. Brian invited her to dinner at his family home in Blacksburg, which was a contemporary house on the side of town furthest from the university, in an expensive subdivision, on a cul-de-sac.

Dinner was brought in by servants, then they discreetly retired. Obviously, that was pre-planned, but Naomi didn't mind. They drank a bottle of wine with dinner, then he gave her a tour of the house. It ended with his bedroom upstairs.

One minute he had just opened the door, and she was admiring the interesting color choices. The next minute he had her against the wall and was kissing her, murmuring that he'd been having trouble keeping his hands off her long enough to eat.

Sex with Brian was — well — adequate was the only word to describe it. Naomi didn't get nearly as much pleasure out of it as Brian did. There was no second round, since Brian fell asleep soon afterwards.

But this time, aware that she was dreaming when she glanced quickly over to the corner where her doctor stood, she was disquieted by the lustful look he was giving her.

Am I imagining things? Is his arm moving? What the fuck? Is he fondling himself while he watches? Yuck!

Peering in through the window, Laird Duncan McLeod wasn't watching Naomi and Brian on the bed. He'd seen them in bed before, both as they were actually doing the deed and in her memories. He was watching the man he'd never seen before, shoving a hand down the front of his pants to stroke himself. Duncan was outraged that anyone, particularly a stranger, would be spying on his creator.

He was rising to climb in the window when he felt a small hand firmly grasp his forearm as a voice whispered in his ear. "No! Don't interfere."

He looked up in surprise to see a female dressed all in black, the fabric clinging to her every curve. She held her finger up to her lips to signal to him to be quiet as she shook her head at him. Her brown curls bounced as her head moved. Her gray eyes narrowed as she settled down next to him to watch the unfolding scene along with him.

Naomi's dream reality took over, creating a montage of scenes of subsequent dates that got steadily more aggravating. The last time she had sex with Brian in his house, she refused to stay the night. She had an early flight out the next morning for a TV interview in Chicago, and she didn't want to chance missing her plane. He argued with her, but she refused.

When he got up out of bed and tried to intimidate her with his size by backing her up against the wall, she lost control over her temper.

"Who the hell do you think you are?"

"I'm your man, and you'll do what I tell you to."

"Oh, really?" Anyone who knew her knew not to irritate her when she got that tone in her voice.

Brian proved he hadn't picked up any knowledge of her moods, any more than he had of what her body enjoyed. "Yes. You're not going anywhere. We're not done here yet."

Naomi stalked over to pick up her discarded clothing and began getting dressed. "Oh, yes, we are. In fact, not only are we done here and now, but I think we're through, Brian. I've had just about enough of you always trying to bully me into doing what you want."

His eyes widened. "Are you breaking up with me?"

"Yes," she barked, pulling on her pants and reaching for her bra.

"But what about us?"

"There is no us, Brian. There's only what you want. It's always about what you want. That's fine. You go on. Keep looking for what you want. I'll head the other way to look for what I want."

"Ellie told me you were independent, but she didn't tell me you were such a bitch."

"Ah, now's the time for the name-calling. When things don't go your way, that's what you resort to? Honestly, Brian. I'm tired of you and your drama. I'm out of here."

Now fully dressed, she strode over to the door and opened it.

"If you walk out that door, we're through. Don't think you can come crawling back."

"Good! And don't hold your breath waiting for me. Goodbye, Brian. I wish I could say it's been fun."

She walked through the door, slamming it behind her, and stomped down the stairs.

The woman adjusted her tight black catsuit to crouch down next to the kilted Scotsman. "See? I told you there wasn't any reason to interfere. This was just a memory of hers. It's already happened. There wasn't any danger to her."

"Ach, lassie, it wasnae her or that sorry excuse for a man Ah was worried aboot. Did ye nae see the stranger? The man in the corner, with his hand doon his trousers?"

"Yeah, I did notice him. I wonder who he is? He can't be one of us, or he'd be watching her from outside of her memories like we do."

"And did ye see him touching himsel'?"

"Well, she is one sexy woman. Too bad she was with that dickless-wonder she's been dating. She's had other men who were more interesting."

"Ye've watched her before?"

"Of course." She studied him closely. "You're her first hero, aren't you? The Scottish Highlander series, right? Laird Duncan."

"Aye. What guv it away, lassie? The kilt? Or me brogue?"

She licked her lips with a hungry look on her face. "Actually, it was the kilt with no shirt on so your wide shoulders and ripped guns are on full display."

He shook his head, his long dark hair swaying gently. "I'm no carryin' any weapons, lassie."

She startled, then grinned. "Guns are your arms, dude. Yours look like they could tear apart a brick wall . . . or lift a car."

"Ah, them things she rides around in instead of on a horse?"

Her lips twitched. "Um, yeah."

"How do ye ken who Ah am, lassie? I dinnae ken you."

"I'm a secret agent . . . it's part of my job. I watch everyone who's in her brain. Though I must say, I agree with her. You're her sexiest hero. That accent? Your brawny, large body? Tell me, sir, what do you have under your kilt?"

His clear blue eyes burned as he appraised her, carefully examining her curves. She knew they were clearly outlined by her outlandish black garb that fit her like a second skin. He looked shocked by her revealing clothing. But her body was calling to him, and he was listening.

"I'd be happy to show ye."

"Would you now?"

"Ach, aye. But what name do ye call yersel'?"

"She's given me a couple of names. The one I use for my job at the agency is Cammy Gardner. My real name is Carmelia Guittierez. But that's too long and ethnic for my occupation. So just call me Cammy."

His brow wrinkled. "Ah'm no familiar with that name. It sounds foreign. Are ye English?"

Her lips twitched. "Yeah. Let's go with that, big guy." She held out her hand. "And speaking of going, let's you and I go back to my place and get to know one another better, shall we?"

He gave her a predatory look as he enclosed her small hand in his large one, and she pulled him back from their viewing perch.

Naomi gasped in a large breath as she woke up from her dream. The doctor was already sitting up, pulling off the electrodes from his head. She reached up to hers. She smelled the faint scent of cedar before a hand appeared in front of her face.

"Please, allow me to help," Will said. "The glue can stick to yer hair, and Ah'd nae see ye hurt for all the tea in China."

Naomi smiled at him. "Okay. Thanks." She turned when the doctor spoke.

"Well, Naomi, I think we can agree that your anxieties and panic attacks have nothing to do with your most recent boyfriend. You seem to have dealt with him quite well. Next time we'll have to delve further back into your memories."

Her eyes narrowed as she responded. "You know, I don't think it has anything to do with any of my exes. I've been thinking about that. I've never had any loud fights or embarrassing scenes with any of them. Since that's what usually sets me off, there must be something else that I've experienced that's causing me to react to the sounds of loud male voices."

He smiled affably at her from behind the desk where he was sitting, typing notes into his laptop. "Why don't you let me be the judge of that, my dear? I am, after all, your doctor, and you're paying me for my opinion and expertise."

She got up and started toward the door. "Fine. I'll see you again on Friday."

He nodded. "In the meantime, you do some thinking about when the first time was that you experienced one of your panic attacks. Where you were? Who else was there? And we'll discuss that before we begin. Good day to you, Naomi."

She turned and walked out of the room. She smiled and nodded at Maggie on the way by since the older woman was on the phone.

After her shower, Naomi pulled on a silk nightgown and settled down in her bed to read. She'd had wine with her take-out dinner and still had half a glass left, so she sipped it as she read about an adventurous spaceship captain who was being seduced by an alien who had more than the usual number of male appendages.

She got so aroused she pulled out her trusty *Steely Stan* from the nightstand drawer and spent some time stimulating her nipples and her clit before she slid him home and brought herself to a satisfying orgasm. She grinned about the fact that it was the sexy black-haired grad student she was imagining at the peak of her pleasure. And when her orgasm left her feeling weak, she wondered if sex with him would be as good — or maybe even better — than what she could imagine. She fell asleep with a smile on her face.

In her dream that night, she observed her characters interacting in ways she'd never imagined. *Oh my! Who is that with Laird Duncan? I know it's him because of his kilt and his long dark hair hanging down his back. If I move close enough, I can watch them. What? It's Cammy! Cammy and Duncan?*

Cammy pulled the Scotsman into her bedroom and reached for his kilt.

His smile was predatory. "Eager, are ye, lassie?"

She nodded at him, her dark eyes almost black with arousal. "Yes. You offered to show me what's under your kilt. I'm waiting."

"I dinnae have to ask what's unna-below yer clothing . . . what little there is of it. But ye'll have to remove it for me first."

She grinned, doing some strip-tease moves as she undid the zipper on the front that ran from her neck down to her pubic area. She pushed her breasts together, showing maximum cleavage, as she bent over slightly, sliding the sleeves off of her toned arms. She lowered the top so that her breasts sprang free.

Duncan made a gutteral sound in his throat, and his blue eyes were glassy as he stared. "Ach, lassie, have ye no shame?"

She shook her head. "Nope. When I want, I get what I want. And right now, I want you."

She pulled him closer, and their lips met in a savage kiss, a brutalizing of their lips as they both expressed strong desires. Her hands took the measure of his bare shoulders, then traveled up to his hair as she reached up to pull his head closer to her.

His hands were tracing her curves, roaming all over her body, up and down her back. Then he cupped her butt in both of his big hands and pulled her up to grind his erection against her mons.

Her feet were off the floor, so she wrapped her legs around his hips, pressing herself against his hardness, riding him through their clothing until she cried out from her quickie orgasm.

His eyes looked dazed as he staggered over to her bed and fell onto her, pressing her into the mattress. He rolled off to the side long enough to pull off his kilt and toss it onto the floor. His gaze burned into her. "Ye need to be naked now, lassie! Ah cannae wait any longer."

A smile played on her lips as she lifted her butt to ease the suit down to her thighs, then she sat up to peel the rest of the one-piece leotard off her legs. When she had it down to her ankles, she slipped her feet out of it and tossed it next to the discarded kilt. She turned to Duncan, moving to crawl on top of him.

He pushed her over. "Ah telt ye, lassie, Ah cannae wait any longer. Ye've driven me mad with yer brazen ways." He knelt in between her thighs, spreading them wider to accommodate his size, and he pushed his hips forward to bury his cock inside of her.

Cammy grunted with the force of his impact. He was so large it bordered on painful for her — it was certainly uncomfortable — at least until her body responded with more natural lubrication. To aid in that and increase her own pleasure, she reached both hands up to twist and pull on her nipples.

Duncan was pounding into her like a machine, his eyes wild and unseeing as he neared his climax. Suddenly he lifted her hips off the bed and howled, gluing her hips to his rigid body, as his orgasm pulsated into her with so much force, she expected to be able to taste it. Then he fell forward onto her once again.

Her breath whooshed out of her as the sudden weight pressed her onto the mattress. They lay quietly for some time while she ran her fingernails up and down his back, playing with the curve of his butt, and smiling. When her need for more oxygen overrode her desire to not move, she gently pushed at his shoulder to get him to roll onto his back.

He let out a long sigh as he rolled over to lie next to her.

She pushed his arm up and crept closer to him, laying her head on his shoulder and fondling the thick hair that covered his chest and abdomen. She pressed herself against his thigh and rubbed, enjoying making herself squeak with small twitching orgasms. Then she smiled, saying gently, "You're an animal! Ready for round two yet?" When he didn't answer, she raised her head up to look into his face.

At that point, he inhaled, then let out a loud snore.

She hissed out her disapproval. "You're asleep?"

CHAPTER FIVE

When Naomi woke the next morning, the first thing she did was smile. *Wow! What a dream! I'd never have thought of putting the two of them together. But she's a wild woman in bed, and he's so hot! Though how could I do that when they're separated by so many centuries?*

She did some stretching as she continued to ponder what her muse had recently shown her. She'd had enough dreams that led to novels for her to know better than to ignore scenes that suggested a story. *I wonder how that could happen? Maybe a time-travel romance? Either she could get stuck in some machinery and get sent back to his century. Or he could be cursed by a witch he'd rejected and get sent into our time. Hmm.*

Since she had no plans for the day, she went out for a leisurely breakfast, taking her e-reader with her so she'd have a book to read as she enjoyed her bacon and swiss cheese omelet. She got involved with her book and lingered over repeated cups of the rich coffee while she sat in the window. She enjoyed the feel of the sun on her skin, warming her almost as much as the sexy story she was reading.

When she finally got back to her apartment, part of the day was spent talking to her agent, dealing with promoting her books, answering emails from her readers, and doing the thousand and one things authors have to do to get and keep their books in front of the reading public.

By mid-afternoon, she was ready to write. Her current work-in-progress was a stand-alone book whose characters had been presented to her in a dream she'd had a few weeks ago. But on a whim, she opened a blank page and started to recreate the hot, steamy scene she'd watched in her sleep last night. But when she tried to backtrack and figure out how to begin the story, she only got a few paragraphs down before her creativity hit a wall. Then she tried to write the scene directly following the sexy one, and once again, she felt writer's block halting her progress.

Well, I guess I'll have to wait to work on that one. I'll have to ponder it for a while, letting the scenes come to me gradually. I can't force them, so I'll have to be patient. I think I need to do some exercising to free up my mind to listen.

She changed into running shorts and a t-shirt and brought a bottle of water with her over to her treadmill. She got onto it and used the remote next to it to turn on her stereo system, cranking it up so she could enjoy her favorite running mix. She pressed the buttons, and the treadmill began to move. She kept increasing the speed and the incline until she had to stop thinking about anything at all except for her deep breathing that allowed her cells to get enough oxygen to keep her running for the mileage she'd pre-chosen as her goal for this week.

Afterward, she took a long, hot shower to relax her muscles. She was still drying herself off with a large fluffy towel when her cell phone rang. She looked around the room, then realized she'd left it near the treadmill. She ran out, wrapping herself in the towel as she moved quickly enough to answer the call before it went to message.

"Hello?"

"Hi, darling. I hope I'm not interrupting anything."

"Mom! No. I was just getting out of the shower after I got done on the treadmill. What's up?"

"Nothing, really. But I haven't seen you for a while. And I'm interested in hearing all about the dream-therapy doctor that your father got you set up with. Can we meet for dinner?"

"Dad, too?"

"No, he's got a business dinner with a client. Besides, we

can't *girl-talk* when he's there, right?"

"Yeah, you're right. Where do you want to go? And when?"

"How soon can you be ready?"

"I can probably be out the door in a half-hour. That gives me time to do something with my hair and throw on some makeup."

"How about that new steakhouse in town? I was there with your father once and ordered the prime rib because they only have that on weekends. But I also want to try their filet. They've got lots of toppings, and you know how I do love me some blue cheese and cracked pepper on a good steak."

Naomi smiled. "Okay, Mom. I'll meet you there about six-thirty, okay? Do we need reservations?"

"I'll make them, sweetie. See you soon."

"Love you, Mom. Thanks for thinking of me."

"Always. Bye."

After a very enjoyable dinner, during which they discussed family members who had weddings, baby showers, and birthdays coming up as well as the outlandish and creative excuses her mother's current group of freshman students kept coming up with for not doing their geology homework, Naomi smiled at her mother when there was a lull in the conversation.

Her mom leaned forward. "So now, what happens in your dream-therapy appointments? Your father has tried to learn more from his golfing buddy, but he's never been to this therapist, so he has no idea. "

"Well, there are two men in the office when I get there. The doctor himself, who between you and me, I think is kind of a dirty old man—and his grad student."

Her mother shook her head. "Oh, dear. At least you're not alone with the doctor, then. Is the grad student female?"

"No, Mom, he's a Scotsman in a kilt."

"What? Just like your hero in your Highlander series?"

"Yes. The first time I met him, he told me that his mom and sisters have read all of my books, but he wanted to let me know that I've got the accent for Duncan all wrong. Seems that with the last name of MacLeod, he's from northern Scotland, while the accent I've been giving him is more from the south, like around Glasgow. Go figure, huh? Who knew there was more than one Scottish accent?"

"Well, dear, I suppose it's like the regional differences here. In Boston, they *pahk the cah*. While here in the south, we ask *how y'all doin' tedaye*?"

Naomi nodded. "Yeah, I guess so. And that first time I met him, he was wearing a kilt! A real-live Scotsman with black hair, pale skin, and freckles, wearing a kilt."

"Hmm, are you perhaps attracted to this grad guy?"

"Mom! I can't be. He's my therapist. Or at least my therapy assistant. I'm sure he's got to follow the same rules as the doctor. You don't canoodle with your patients. It's not allowed."

"Pity, seeing as how you've always been so attracted to men with accents. And your best-selling hero wears a kilt. I suppose your grad student was wearing a shirt with it? It's kind of chilly yet for him to be walking around like your laird, wearing a kilt and nothing else."

Naomi's lips twitched in amusement. "Yes, Mom, He had on a shirt and jacket, kind of like a formal suit, I guess. But the doctor told him to tone his accent down, and he's been wearing jeans and a t-shirt ever since."

"Aw, that's too bad. I was hoping he'd inspire you to write another of your Laird Duncan books. It's been years since your last one."

"You know I've been enjoying writing my Cammy Gardner spy novels lately. But I may have a new idea kicking around in my head."

"You know, dear, just because you can't date the grad student doesn't mean you can't be friendly. I mean, if you were to run into him in a coffee shop, you could sit and chat with him for a while, couldn't you? That wouldn't be against any rules. You'd be in a public place. Or if you went for a walk in the park or got ice cream together. You could make friends with him. Then when your therapy is done, you'd be halfway there already, right?"

"Mom! I don't want to get him into any kind of trouble."

"Of course not, darling. And neither do I. So how, exactly, do these sessions happen? Are you hypnotized to sleep? Or are you just so dazzled by the sexy Scotsman that you swoon into a deep sleep?"

Naomi laughed along with her mom, then spent some time explaining the procedure while they had dessert.

It was quite late when they finally left the restaurant. They got in a few close hugs before parting. When Naomi got home, she was tired enough to just slip into her nightgown and crawl into bed with her e-reader. She was still reading about the alien with tentacles.

Why doesn't my brain give me interesting ideas like that? I'd sure like to write something outlandish like a sci-fi alien romance. Oh well. Gotta write what the muse gives me, I guess.

She fell asleep while reading.

And when she woke up, she was quite disappointed that she'd had no interesting dreams that night. But since she had a morning book reading in a library, followed by a book signing scheduled for the afternoon, she didn't have time to mope about it. She got dressed, ate her breakfast, and headed out for another long day of smiling and getting writer's cramp while signing her name so many times it would start to look like someone else's name. *And since it isn't my real name, it actually* is *someone else's name.*

CHAPTER SIX

Fortunately, there were no arguments during the book signing this time, so after it was over, Naomi was tired but in a good mood. She picked up a quick dinner of soup and salad from the local *Panera*, then headed back to try to do some writing.

She sat and stared at what she'd written already. The images from her dream of her two lead characters having an encounter were steamy. But try as she might, she had no ideas on how they ended up having sex or how they would act toward each other after. With a sigh, she did some minor editing on her website, then decided to read herself to sleep again. She finished the alien romance, then turned out her light with an enormous yawn. She soon fell asleep.

She had no idea how long she'd been asleep when the scenery changed. She looked around, realizing she was in the apartment of her favorite heroine, Cammy Gardner, the infamous secret agent who always got her man. "Or men, as in the last book," she reminded herself with a smile.

"Hey, girl, you and me, we need to talk." Cammy was pouring wine into two glasses. She handed one to Naomi.

"What about?"

"You can't write me into a time-travel romance."

"No? Why not? I'm the writer. I can write whatever I want."

Cammy lifted one shapely eyebrow. "Oh really? Well then, I guess you don't need me showing you any of my life scenes anymore. I'll just be quiet and let you do all of the work."

Naomi was dismayed. "No! I need you to show me images. That's where I get all of my good ideas."

Cammy smirked. "I know."

"You don't want me to write a time-travel romance starring you and Duncan? But you two looked so hot together! You're always glad to seduce sexy men, and he's always been my not-so-secret crush."

Cammy's lips twitched. "Please don't."

"Why?"

Cammy sighed. "When you write his character, you try to be true to the time period he lives in, right?"

"I do my best."

"Well . . . so did he. But it wasn't world-shaking for me."

"What?"

"Good God, girl, the man has no idea what foreplay is! I doubt he's ever even heard of a clit. He certainly didn't know how to do anything for it. He was all wham-bam-thank-you-ma'am. Then he was snoring."

Naomi drank her wine, trying to process her shock. "But when I write his books, he never disappoints the ladies. They're always happy with him."

"Yeah, but they're from the same time period, right? And virgins? So they don't expect anything more from him than he's able to give."

She leaned over and patted the back of Naomi's hand. "Look, you and I are modern, independent women. We expect a man to know his way around the female body. Not all of them do, of course. But most at least have some idea of what's involved with foreplay. That guy? No idea. I mean, don't get me wrong, he's Major Studly in that kilt. And no shirt means his rock-hard abs and great guns are on display for you to drool over. And what he's got under his kilt? It's a caber!"

They both laughed.

Cammy pointed to her TV, which was suddenly turned on and showing an excerpt from the recent Highland games. The event showing was the tossing of the caber. A brawny man in a kilt was struggling to lift what looked like a telephone pole upright, then he gave it a heave, tossing it so that it hit the ground with one end, then flipped over to hit the other end.

Naomi sipped her wine again. "Okay. No time-travel romance for you. But maybe I could write it, just with a different heroine?"

Cammy snorted. "Make sure she's a virgin, so she won't know any better."

Naomi giggled. "Or maybe an older woman, who'd be glad to instruct him in the ways of love?"

"I don't know. He's pretty alpha. He might not take kindly to being told he's in need of lessons in the art of love-making."

"Okay. Are you going to give me any new plot ideas for your next book?"

"Soon, probably. I've got so many adventures you haven't written yet that you'll never run out of stories to write about me."

Naomi sat back, more relaxed.

"But I've gotta ask you, who's that weird old bald dude with the beard who's been lurking around in your daydreams?"

Naomi grinned. "He's a dream-therapist. He claims he can help me figure out why I've been getting panic attacks in public or feeling anxiety around couples fighting and yelling. It's happened enough times that I'm concerned about it. I don't want to take drugs for it because I'm afraid that might interfere with my writing."

Cammy nodded. "I see. So he's observing you while you dream?"

"No, he's observing me while I revisit memories, in a light dream state, during the day. He's certain that I've got something buried away that I don't want to remember. He thinks that once he helps me to find it, we can . . . like, pull a shade up . . . and I'll see it. Then I can deal with it, and I won't have issues anymore." Naomi leaned forward. "Wait a minute! Is that how you and Duncan ended up together?"

"Yeah. We were both watching him in your memories, wondering who the hell he was. We take care of you in here, you know. You're our only way to exist. Without you writing our stories, we'd be stuck in your mind. When you write about us and your fans read about us, then we can live in their heads, also. So anything that concerns you in here concerns us, too."

"So you'll let him know not to worry about the doctor?"

"Sure. But what about the other guy?"

"What other guy?"

"The black-haired younger man. He wore a kilt once. But he's been in jeans ever since."

"The grad student? He's not supposed to be in my head. He told me that he just runs the machine that allows the doctor access to my memories."

Cammy shrugged. "Well, he's in here, too, whenever the doctor is. Only he lurks in the corner, in a shadow and out of sight. I don't think the doctor realizes he's in here. Duncan never mentioned him, so he probably didn't see him. You haven't seemed to notice, either. But you know how observant I am. I have to be in my line of work."

"Hmm. I'll have to ask him. But since he's not supposed to be in my head, I'll have to try to get him alone. I don't want him to get into any trouble."

Cammy's lips twitched again. "Oh, I'm sure you'll enjoy getting him alone, won't you? You and your guys-in-kilts-thing."

Naomi could feel her face getting hot as she blushed. "Yeah, he really is one sexy dude. Especially when he's wearing his kilt. But he's part of my therapy team, so he's not allowed to date me."

"Then the sooner you get this problem of yours taken care of, the sooner you can be free to date the sexy kilted man who's from our time. So, hopefully, he knows about foreplay."

"I sure hope so."

They shared a very female grin of understanding.

"Ciao, babe."

Naomi woke up to her alarm clock ringing. She reached over and hit at it, so the snooze would give her a few minutes more. She lay back and smiled.

Well, at least now I know why I was having writer's block. I'll have to save that scene, just in case I do decide to write a time-travel romance starring Laird Duncan.

Her brow furrowed. *But how am I ever going to get Will alone to ask him about his intruding into my dreams when the doctor does? I'll have to be extra attentive today. I just hope that if I do see him, it won't alert the doctor to his being there. I have a feeling that he keeps to the shadows so Dr. Alan won't notice him there. I wonder why?*

She kept on pondering while she got dressed, ate a quick breakfast, then headed out the door for her next dream-therapy appointment.

CHAPTER SEVEN

When Naomi walked in the door for her Friday appointment, Maggie was on the phone with a patient. She smiled and waved for Naomi to sit.

After a few minutes, Maggie hung up. She reached under her desk and pulled out a small bag with a few more books.

Naomi smiled and moved closer to sign the books for her ardent fan. She was on the last book when the phone system buzzed.

Maggie nodded. "They're ready for you now, Naomi. And thanks so much for being so sweet about signing even my older books."

Naomi grinned. "It's the least I can do for such an ardent fan. I wish I had a new book coming out so I could give you an advance copy. But I promise the next book I get a contract for, you'll get your copy of it when I get mine. You won't have to wait for it to hit the stores."

Maggie's eyes shone. "That would be wonderful!"

Naomi turned and went into the therapy room.

As usual, Will was tinkering with the machine while the doctor was sitting at his desk, perusing some paperwork.

"Does it need to be constantly adjusted?" Naomi inclined her head when Will looked up at her.

He shook his head. "It's nae that. But it's temperamental, it is. Sometimes it's like the wires move themsel's around when we're nae here."

The doctor approached them. "Now, Will, I keep telling you that's not possible. Maybe the cleaning people dust the machine, and that's how things get moved around. Either way, you always manage to get it to work, so there's no harm done, right?"

Will nodded. "Ach aye. Yer right."

"Good. Then we're ready to proceed?" He turned to watch Naomi slipping off her shoes and sitting down on her chair.

"I guess."

Dr. Alan sat on the other chair and turned to Naomi. "Today, I thought we should revisit some of your college memories. I don't know if you were a wild woman in college or not. Some people do act out when they're living on their own for the first time."

Naomi shook her head. "Not me. During my freshman year, two of my brothers were on the campus at the same time. They had their friends all keeping an eye on me. Made it damn near impossible for me to get laid at all."

There was a quick snort of laughter that was quickly suppressed as Will ducked his head down quickly, as if he had to adjust something below the machine.

The doctor continued as if he hadn't noticed the interruption. "Well, even so, the first time living out of the house, the easy access to alcohol and illegal drugs . . . all of that can make the perfect recipe for an occurrence that might not be remembered consciously, but might be what we're looking for."

"So we're going even further back into my memories?"

"Yes. The process is still the same, but I'll have to interact with you more in order to walk you back through the years. That's why we're discussing it now. So you already know where we're going to go in your memories."

Will walked over to apply the wires to Naomi's head.

She grinned up at him.

Startled, he returned her smile. Then his eyes concentrated on where he needed to position the electrodes.

Naomi inhaled deeply, as if she was trying to relax. In

reality, she was enjoying the cedar aroma that seemed to be a part of the sexy Scotsman.

Dr. Alan handed the bottle of scented oil to Will before he started to apply the electrodes to his own skull.

Naomi breathed in the odor of the calming lavender and started to consciously slow her breathing. Deep breaths in — even deeper breaths out.

Will walked over to check that all of the doctor's wires were attached correctly, then he went over to his customary place behind the machine.

"Are we ready then?" Dr. Alan addressed them both.

Will softly replied, "Aye, sir."

Naomi nodded, then began to chant the repetitious syllables with the doctor until she felt herself drift off.

Naomi looked around, smiling as she breathed in deeply, the perfume of summer flowers overwhelming. She had always enjoyed her summers spent on campus instead of having to return home. She even took a class each summer, fitting in things her schedule normally wouldn't have let her choose — like the art class that she took between her sophomore and junior years. She knew that was when she'd landed when she glanced down at her hands and saw the clay under her fingernails. She'd enjoyed that Introduction to 3-D Art class.

She'd enjoyed her professor even more. She smiled, remembering the flirting that went on all summer, until the class was finally over, and she managed to seduce the sexy artist who'd starred in her fantasies for weeks.

"Good memories?"

She jumped, having forgotten that Dr. Alan was going to be conversing with her this time.

"Um, yes. My older brother had graduated by this time, and the other brother was so involved with the guy he was dating that he didn't waste any time keeping tabs on me. Plus, he and I are closer in age, so he didn't feel so responsible for me. He actually trusted me

to be able to take care of myself."

"Which you did?"

"Yes. I had a summer three-D Art class that I really enjoyed."

"Let's go to one of your classes."

"Sure."

With the suddenness of the dreamscape, she looked around to see that they were in the classroom. Naomi was perched on a chair that was higher than usual to be able to reach the top of the higher table. She stared at the professor as he waved his arms around, describing the new assignment, showing examples of the slab pieces made by former students, and demonstrating the techniques he wanted them all to learn.

Dr. Alan spoke into her ear. "You enjoyed more than the class, didn't you?"

She turned to look at him in surprise.

He grinned. "Your heart rate and your respirations have both sped up. In fact, even your eyes are glassy. You bad girl. Did you have an affair with your professor?"

"Not until after the class was over," she responded indignantly. "He was difficult to convince, even then."

"But you enjoyed each other after he was no longer your teacher?"

"Yes. And really, dude, there are no bad memories from my college days that I'm aware of. So I think we're in the wrong place."

"Show me more."

There was a slow montage of scenes — Naomi drinking with her friends in the college town bars. Naomi in bed with the professor at his home, which was filled with art pieces that he'd collected over the years. Naomi in class — giving speeches — reading her poetry. Naomi with her brother and some friends, spending the day floating around on tubes at a local river.

The next scenes were her new classes for junior year. The minutia of her days involved getting up early for some classes and sleeping in on alternating days. She attended classes — she met friends in bars or in coffeehouses — she seemed to be enjoying herself in mostly all of the memories.

One of them that she hadn't enjoyed so much involved a blind date she'd been set up with. The guy didn't tell her he was taking her to a local bar that had a wet t-shirt night. Once she realized what was happening on the stage, she'd excused herself to go to the bathroom soon after the entertainment *started, and snuck out the back door. She'd had a long walk home, but it was still a warm night, and she was happy to have ditched the guy who was so wrong for her.*

But while she was still sitting there, watching as the guy she was with yakked it up with his friends who were there, too, ogling the girls on the stage, she glanced over at her doctor to find his eyes glassy as he joined the other men in the bar, staring at the busty girls providing the scenery.

Figures. I get a therapist who's a dirty old man. As long as he keeps his hands off me, I guess it doesn't matter. And there's always Will in the room with us.

She suddenly remembered that she was supposed to look for him. She glanced around the room, paying particular attention to the darker corners. There was a couple smooching and groping in the first place she looked, so she moved her focus around the room, looking for black hair.

There! Is that him? *She peered more closely at the shadowy figure that was hard to see clearly. Everyone else there was easy to see, but the lines of his body were blurry and indistinct. She wondered if he was doing something to make himself harder to see.*

She kept staring at him until his face turned and his eyes met hers.

He startled, then became even more blurry, as if he was being covered by smoke or fog.

Even knowing he was there, soon she was unable to see anything to suggest that there was a man there, let alone someone she knew.

How odd.

Then it was time for her to excuse herself, remembering that the guys were all too busy staring at the perky nipples to even notice that she was leaving.

Dr. Alan appeared at her elbow again. "So your junior and senior years of college were also uneventful?"

"Yup. I told you, I think we're in the wrong time frame. I really enjoyed myself when I was living in a college town. So whatever we're looking for must have happened way before this."

Naomi felt the slide of time passing, and soon she opened her eyes and looked around, blinking.

She watched as Dr. Alan sat up, pulling off his electrodes. The whiff of cedar let her know that Will had approached her, and a second later, his hands were removing her electrodes as well. She tried to smile at him, but this time he avoided looking into her eyes.

Once again, she thought *how odd.*

Dr. Alan walked over to seat himself behind his desk again. His laptop was open, and he began to type into it. When he saw that Will was finished removing all of her wires, he waved at the seat on the other side of his desk.

Naomi walked over and sat down. "So you agree with me? It's not something from my college years?"

He nodded. "Probably not. You seem to have been a normal, healthy, red-blooded female enjoying the freedom of living away from home for the first time. No, my dear, I think we'll have to delve even further into your past. Next time we'll tackle your high school years. If we're still unsuccessful, then we'll head into your middle and grade school years."

"So that's, what, three more visits?"

He arched his brows. "I'm sure you have memories from before you started school, as well. Most people do, but they're the hardest to access."

"When I was just a little kid? How could something that happened so long ago be affecting me now?"

"It depends on what the event was that has lurked in your subconscious all of these years and is now wreaking havoc with your equanimity. And sometimes the memory that's causing the most trouble is one that's hardest to access. We'll just have to keep on delving into your background until we find the event that frightened you so much that you're working hard not to remember it."

Naomi shrugged. "Okay, I guess. So I need to make two appointments for next week also?"

"Why don't you go ahead and make four more appointments? That will get us through to your toddler years. If it's any earlier than that, it will be impossible to access. Most human beings are just not equipped to remember things from our infancy. I suspect it has to do with not having words to tie those memories to, but that's only one theory."

Naomi got up, slipped her shoes back on, and went out of the office to set up the next appointments.

When she was done, she walked out into the sunshine of a late spring day. While it didn't smell as good as her memories of a summer day on the campus where she'd attended college, it was still nice to inhale deeply and smell flowers, rather than just cold that made her nose sting.

It's such a nice day I think I'll go grab a coffee at that place here on the campus. It'll be crowded, but then it usually is. And I'm not going to eat there—just get a mocha latte and maybe sit outside to enjoy it.

It only took her about fifteen minutes to get to the coffeehouse. The line wasn't as long as she'd feared, and the baristas kept it moving. It was still sunny and bright, despite being late afternoon, when she moved out onto the patio to look for a seat. Since there weren't any open, she casually strolled toward the nearby park, meaning to try to find a bench there. Just as she moved past one of the patio tables, the three guys there got up and headed off. She quickly grabbed one of their chairs and sat down at the table, immensely pleased with her good luck.

She was sitting facing the entrance of the coffeehouse, enjoying the feel of the warm sunshine on her face. She closed her eyes briefly. She opened them again to take another sip of her caffeinated confection. As she glanced up, she saw Will coming out of the door, beginning to search for a place to sit.

She waved her hand at him, trying to catch his eye.

When he noticed her, his eyes lit up.

The smile on his face warmed her even more than the sunshine. As he approached her, she teased him. "Are you following me, mister?"

He looked startled. "Um, no? Ah come here to do ma homework after ma job with the doctor is done."

She waved to indicate the chairs at the table, and he appeared initially reluctant, but a quick glance around confirmed that there weren't any other open seats to be had. He sat down across from her. "What are *you* doin' here?"

Naomi shrugged. "I like their mochas. Not too sweet, and they use a really primo dark chocolate. They even put little shavings on top of the whipped cream." She took another sip of her drink before smiling at him.

Will stared at her lips.

Naomi's tongue shot out to lick off the cream and the tiny chocolate pieces that had stuck to her upper lip. "There. That better?"

His eyes were an intense blue as he silently nodded.

"You don't look happy to see me. Why?"

He took a deep breath. "Ah'm part of yer therapy team. Ah cannae be seen fraternizin' with a patient. It's nae allowed."

"Why not? I mean, it's not like we're having a private tryst, are we?" She gave him a flirty look before waving her hands around. "We're in a public place, surrounded by lots of other people. Surely we can be friends, can't we?"

He shook his head. "It's nae allowed."

She rolled her eyes. "Stupid rules." She leaned forward. "Actually, I'm hoping to listen to you talking long enough so that I'll be able to be more accurate in my depiction of my Highlander hero."

His lips twitched in a grin that gave his face a boyish look. "Ah telt ye, lassie, yer laird isnae a Glaswegian. He's from the north country. So ma brogue willnae do ye any good."

She grinned back at him. "Okay. Then can I just sit and enjoy your accent? I've always been a sucker for Scottish brogues."

He raised one brow. "Oh? Have ye ever been to the auld country?"

"Only once with my parents when I was in high school. We spent a couple of weeks one summer, starting in London, then moving north to Scotland. I remember being thrilled with all of the castles, drafty as they might be, and I loved watching the pageantry of the guards at Buckingham Palace." She leaned toward him again, speaking in a conspiratorial lower tone. "Tell me, is it true what they say, that there's a mirror on the floor close to the exit from the changing room, so that someone is supposed to check to be sure that the guards are wearing the proper — um — undergarments under their kilts?"

Will blushed as he chuckled. "Aye, lassie, 'tis. There are often pictures published in the local rag-mags showin' what happens when a sudden wind blows up the kilt, and the man is caught flashin' the photographer . . . and anyone else around, too."

Naomi smiled broadly. "So, is that traditional? I mean, it can get very cold in Scotland. When I was there, even though it was summer, it was still chilly at night."

"Ach aye, it's traditional. After all, authentic kilts are made of heavy wool, which can be verra hot when the weather gets too warm."

"The kilt you were wearing the first time I met you didn't look that heavy."

"Ach, that's true. But Ah was wearin' what the website called *an everyday kilt*, made of a polyester and wool blend. So it wasnae as heavy as a traditional kilt. It also wasnae the

Hamilton tartan neither."

"Oh, that's right. Every clan has a tartan of their own, right?"

"Aye, lassie. And some of the larger clans, like the Stewarts or the McDonalds, have more than one tartan, depending on which branch of the clan ye were descended from."

"But your family, the Hamiltons, only has one tartan?"

He nodded. "Aye. It's a red dominant, with three stripes o' blue close together and a thinner white stripe."

"I'd love to see you in your full formal dress wearing your proper tartan kilt. I'll bet you really look good in it."

Will's blush darkened, which was made all the more visible by his very pale skin.

"Oh, I'm sorry. I didn't mean to embarrass you. Was that too personal of a comment to make to someone I'm just having coffee with? I told you I really loved the Scottish culture when I was there. That is, after all, how I got the ideas for my very first book I had published. And where I got the idea for Laird Duncan MacLeod."

Will's lips twitched again. "But, lassie, if it's cold enough to be wearin' the kilt, ye'd be a fool to go bare-chested, wouldn't ye?"

Naomi smiled back at him. "I suppose so. But it's a *romance* novel, dude. We women aren't as visual as you men are, but we still like to look at a well-built man's chest. In fact, that's probably why your mom and sisters read my books. There's always a sexy man on the cover. Gives them someone to fantasize about while they read."

"And yer no embarrassed about the view into yer mind that ye give to yer readers?"

Naomi sat back, her eyes widening. "What do you mean?"

Will shifted around as if suddenly uncomfortable. "Well, Ah havenae read any of yer books, but Ah've paged through them when Ah found them lyin' aroon the hoose. They're, uh, explicit."

Naomi felt her lips twitching now. "Of course they are! That's what most romance readers want. They want to be swept off their feet by a romantic hero who falls so deeply in love with the heroine that he'll do anything to protect her, or to win her love, if she's hard to convince. And when they finally do get to fall into bed, the whole idea is to satisfy the readers as much as the characters."

Warming to her topic, Naomi continued. "And what few men seem to realize is that they don't have to ask that perennial question anymore about what it is that women want. All they have to do is pick up a romance novel, preferably one of mine, and read it. That will tell them all they need to know about how to satisfy a woman."

Will blushed again, an even darker shade of red.

She leaned back to shake her head. "Now I've embarrassed you again. I'm sorry." She thought for a minute. "No, I'm not. I'd like to go on a date with you, Mr. Will Hamilton. But I know that you're not allowed to date me while I'm a patient, even though you're not my therapist."

"Ah'm part of the therapy team."

"Yes, you are. So that means that the sooner I can pinpoint what memory is giving me trouble, the sooner we can go on a real date. I think we both want that to happen, don't we?"

This time Will nodded through his faint blush. "Aye, that's the truth of it, lassie."

"Well then, we can be friends meeting for coffee for now. That way, once we're free to date, we'll already be friends. So we'll both be ready for more. Right?"

She was gratified by the look of lust that flitted quickly across the face of the man as his eyes gleamed at her.

"Aye."

Naomi jumped when her phone rang. "Darn it!" She fished it out of her purse and glanced at it while it was still ringing.

"It's my mom. I have to answer it."

* * Will nodded to acknowledge her before he opened his laptop. He pretended to be working but he listened intently to the half of the conversation that he could hear.

"Hi, Mom, what's up?"

She listened, then spoke again. "Gramma misses us and wants us to visit her? At her place? Yes, I know she doesn't get much time off. This weekend? No, I don't have any other plans. Okay, tell her I'll be glad to get to eat her cooking again. Yes, I suppose I can stay with you there until Monday. But I've got a therapist's appointment on Tuesday, so I've got to be home by Monday night. Okay, great. I'll head home now and figure out what I have to do to clear up a couple of days on my schedule. Who's driving? You or me? You just want to relax? Fine, I'll drive. What time?"

She listened, then responded. "Oh, you have to work late tonight? So we should grab brunch tomorrow before leaving town? Okay. Yes, I'm excited about seeing Gramma again."

She put down her phone and looked up to see that Will was staring at her.

He felt himself blush again at being caught.

"Sorry, but I've got to cut our visit short."

"Ah know. Ah heard. Ye run along now, lassie. Enjoy yer weekend with yer family."

"Maybe we can have coffee again next Tuesday after my appointment?"

He nodded. "Maybe."

She smiled. "I hope so. It was nice getting to actually talk to you. You're an interesting man, Will."

She got up, then was surprised when Will got up, also. "Are you leaving, too?"

He shook his head. "No, Ahm stayin' to do some homework."

She smiled at him. "Oh, so you're just being a polite man by getting up when I do? You don't have to be so formal with me, Will. We're friends, after all, right?"

He nodded, his clear blue eyes watching her closely.

"Okay, then. Have a good weekend, and I'll see you again on Tuesday."

She picked up her cup and swallowed the last of her coffee. Then she turned and moved smoothly through the crowd, tossing her cup as she passed a garbage can.

Will's gaze was glued to her every move. *Ach, lassie. Ye have no idea what being this close to ye was doin' to me. Ah've no been able te concentrate on anythin' since meetin' ye. An' Ah'm wantin' so much more than friendship from you.*

He sighed deeply, looking around to check if there was anyone he knew sitting anywhere near him. Satisfied that they hadn't been seen by anyone who might report their sitting at the same table having coffee, he positioned his laptop on the table in front of him and dove into his homework.

CHAPTER EIGHT

After having thoroughly enjoyed being able to drive at high speed on the highway, Naomi smiled in recognition as she pulled off the two-lane road onto the driveway that led up to the antebellum mansion that had been her second home when she was a very young child.

Her mother seemed to have the same reaction. "I always enjoy this first view of the mansion, don't you?"

Naomi nodded. "But I like seeing Gramma's cozy cottage even more, where I spent so many happy times with her."

"It was always such a relief for me that she was willing to have you stay with her during the school year when your brothers weren't around to babysit for their baby sister. Your father and I both had to work long hours back then. The housekeeper was home, of course, and that was enough over-sight for your brothers when they got home from school. But I didn't want you growing up with a nanny watching you. I wanted it to be someone who loved you."

"And I loved being here. Gramma would take me up to *the big house* when she had to cook, and I would sit in the kitchen and color pictures while she cooked. Sometimes she'd let me help her mix things. She even taught me how to bake cookies, remember?"

"Yes. It was so cute when you'd come home and ask me to get the ingredients so you could bake cookies for us, to show off your newly-acquired skills."

Naomi drove past the mansion and headed around the back, driving until they saw the small cottage that held such

59

happy memories for both of them.

"Mom taught me how to bake, also, when I was a kid. It was fun growing up living in this cottage, but having the grounds all around to play on and the Reynolds kids as my playmates."

Naomi deftly parked the car behind the cottage and got out to stretch after the long drive. "There wasn't anyone my age here when I'd come to stay with Gramma."

"No, the ones I'd grown up with were mostly off living their own lives, raising their own kids where they were living."

The back door of the cottage was flung open, and they both turned to smile at the woman holding out her arms to them.

"Come and give me a hug, both of you! Lord a mighty! My arms have been achin' to hug my babies!"

Naomi was closer, so she moved into the outstretched arms of the woman who used to be so tall in her memories but who now looked her in the eyes, since they were equal in height. She inhaled the aroma of her gramma, who smelled of vanilla and sugar, along with the comforting and familiar smell of *home.*

"Oh, I've missed you so much, my little Delu!" Gramma murmured loving words at her both in English and in French as she ran her hands all over Naomi's back and arms before kissing her face multiple times.

Naomi smiled from within that tight embrace. "I've missed you too, Gramma. It's been way too long since you've been able to shove my knees under the table and feed me. I'm looking forward to whatever you want me to eat."

They released each other to share a grin.

Naomi's mother moved closer to the circle of love, and her mother embraced her next. "Oh, my darling Marie, my baby girl. How I've missed you!"

"But, Mom, I call you every week!" she defended herself.

"But I can't hug and kiss you over the phone, can I?"

"No, Mom. I miss that, too."

The older woman backed away to wave her arms toward her kitchen. "Come on in, you two. I asked for the night off from cooking for the family, so I've got a special treat for both of you!"

"I thought something smelled really good," Naomi said with a smile. "I mean, besides you. You've been baking, haven't you?"

"Of course! When I get my two favorite girls here, I can't wait to tempt them with some sweet treats!"

Gramma led the way into her kitchen, where Naomi exclaimed, "Mom! She made us a sweet potato pie!"

Naomi's mom groaned. "Mother! You know I always eat more of that than I should. Then I feel guilty for a week."

Gramma shook her head sternly. "Tut, tut. None of that *white-people-guilt* stuff in my house, young lady. It's not a crime to eat delicious foods. It's more of a crime to deprive yourself of tastes you like because you think you're not thin enough the way you are. We know better than that, don't we?" She winked at Naomi.

Naomi nodded, grinning back at her. "We sure do, Gramma. I don't eat as well as I do here in any other place on earth. So since I don't live here, I intend to enjoy myself while I visit. Guilt-free for me!"

At some point, Naomi and Marie brought in their overnight bags and threw them into the spare bedroom. They argued about who would sleep where for a few minutes before Naomi said loudly, "I'm sleeping on the couch in the living room, Mom. That's final! That way I can watch some TV, relax with the light on, and I won't be keeping either of you awake too late."

Her mother had to agree with her logic, so it was settled.

They all moved into the kitchen to yak while Gramma enlisted their help as she needed it in order to whip up a feast more fit for about ten people than for the three of them. When they teased the chef about it, she sternly told them they had to take leftovers home with them, so a little bit of her would travel back with them. That led to some teary eyes, which led to another round of hugs.

Naomi looked around at her surroundings while cutting up fruit for a salad. Her mother was busily mashing the potatoes while Gramma stirred the gravy, and she felt suffused with a warm glow. *Everything around me is so familiar. I feel like I'm in a cocoon of love, with Gramma's happiness at having us both here acting like a dome, keeping us all warm.*

They all ate until they were unable to move, then had pie. At that point, getting up to do the dishes was a welcome diversion to get the blood flowing again and to help in digesting prodigious amounts of food. The happy bustling around in the kitchen was made even more enjoyable when Gramma put on some of her old R&B CDs, and they danced while they packaged up the leftovers and cleaned up the dishes and the counters.

Then Gramma pulled out a deck of cards, and they played games late into the night, enjoying endless cups of herbal teas while they discussed everything going on in their lives to catch up. Then they began discussing the state of the world, and each offered suggestions they could all agree on that would make the world a much more livable, sensible place to enjoy — if only someone would put them in charge.

Finally, when Gramma fell asleep with her cards still in her hands, Naomi and her mom helped her to bed, then retired themselves.

The next morning, Gramma was up well before Naomi wanted to be. But since she was on the couch, there was no way of sleeping through the breakfast preparations or the smell of coffee brewing. She enjoyed having her Gramma to herself for even a small amount of time. Despite the large dinner that they'd all eaten, Gramma insisted on putting a quiche into the oven before she left for her breakfast duties up at the main house.

"Oh, and I forgot to mention to you, but you and your mom are invited to join the Reynolds family for Sunday supper tonight."

"Oh? Why?"

"Because you're a famous author, and they'll be having a small gathering of friends and family, and they want to be able to brag about knowing you."

Naomi rolled her eyes. "Famous? They've known me since, what? Since I was two?"

Gramma gave her a quick hug. "No, you were just turned three when your mom went back to working full-time. That's when she used to leave you out here for extended stays. She'd drive out with your brothers to visit on weekends sometimes. But I was thrilled to be the luckiest gramma around, getting to have my adorable little granddaughter to myself for long stretches of time. Those years before you started school were some of the happiest days of my life."

"I have so many fond memories of being here with you. You taught me how to play cards before I could even read numbers. Remember? I used to have to count the pips on the cards to know which one I was playing."

"Yes, I remember. And I taught you how to bake and how to crochet. And I like to think I was partially responsible for your love of reading, which of course, resulted in your becoming a writer of best-selling novels."

Naomi sighed. "I've never really felt comfortable being in the big house. Especially since *you* have to do all of the cooking, so I won't be able to talk to you much while you're stuck in the kitchen."

Gramma smiled. "But *you* will be the only one who knows that I put love into every mouthful, just for you. And for your mom, too, of course."

"What time will we have to be there?"

"Sunday supper begins at five."

"Then we'll be back here by, what? Seven?"

"Yes, honey. Or soon after that. Then we can spend another delightful night talking and laughing with each other. I rarely get to have a *girls' night*, so I'm thankful for any time I can have with the two girls I love the most in the world."

Gramma looked at her watch. "I've got to run now, Delu. I'll see you after lunch, since I'll be starting on that right after I get done with breakfast. Then I'll have some of the dinner stuff to prep before I can come back for maybe a quick nap. You and your mother can feel free to use or eat anything in my house while I'm gone. And Miss Elizabeth said to tell you that you can walk around the grounds as you please. She said to say this to you . . . *You're* our *guest, too. We welcome you here and look forward to hearing about your exciting career over supper.*"

Naomi's eyebrows rose. "Pretty forward thinking to be so welcoming to the cook's granddaughter."

"Don't think of it that way, honey. They remember when you were living with me here, and you were such an adorable, precious child. Their Hannah used to say that babysitting for you was the highlight of her day."

Naomi watched as a shadow of remembered grief passed quickly over her grandmother's face. "I don't really remember her much. I know she was my babysitter, but I was too young to remember much about her."

"That's fine, honey. They never mention her name, so you won't be asked to share any memories. Now I really have to run. Give me a hug and kiss, and I'll see you later."

Naomi moved into the open arms of her loving gramma. She took her cup of coffee and her phone out onto the porch to sit in a comfortable rocking chair. She watched as Gramma walked along the path that led up to the big house, which was so far away that it wasn't visible from the cottage.

Naomi and her mom enjoyed the quiche along with some leftover fruit salad for their breakfast. After that, they decided that a walk would be a good idea. Many of the bushes were flowering, and the delightful aroma of honeysuckle flowers and magnolia trees in full bloom kept them company as they strolled along the path. Partway up, they took a side trail that led to a playground that appeared to be long-forgotten. The grass was longer around the area, as if no one wanted to visit it, so it was being left to return to its natural state.

"Do you remember playing here when you were young, darling?"

"Not really, Mom. I mean, I remember the swings. Their daughter, who was my babysitter, must have put me into the baby swings, because I don't think I'd have been old enough for the regular swings. I've always liked that back-and-forth movement. It's so soothing . . . like being on a rocker."

"Race you to the swings."

They both giggled as they tore off toward the swings. Since her mother had been closer, she was the first one onto a swing, and she promptly began to pedal her legs furiously. Naomi climbed onto the swing next to her mom, and they enjoyed swinging as high as they could and jumping off, only to get right back onto their swings again.

Marie was horrified when Naomi showed off her favorite move, leaning backward and dragging her long hair in the dirt. "Naomi Delu Morrison! You stop that right now!"

"Why, Mom? I've always done this on swings."

Her mom shuddered. "Not where I could see."

"Oh, well then. I guess it wasn't dangerous as long as my mom couldn't see it, huh? It's part of how my brothers taught me to live dangerously."

Marie had stopped swinging and moved over to the dilapidated picnic table to sit on the table with her feet on the bench.

"Ew, Mom, there's more bird poo on that table than paint."

"That's why I'm sitting up on the table part. It looks cleaner and more sturdy."

Naomi stayed on the swing, moving to sit sideways on it so she could continue to rock back-and-forth, but sideways.

"You know, I've always been sorry that we didn't give you a sister, Naomi."

Naomi shrugged. "Why? I never noticed a lack. I had three big brothers to amuse me. Granted, when I was really small, they didn't know what to do with me. But once I got older, I got to do lots of fun stuff with them that a sister probably wouldn't have wanted to do."

"Like what?"

"Anything. Racing bikes down hills. Sledding down the highest hills we could find. Skitching on the backs of cars while on a skateboard. Climbing trees up as high as we could, then jumping off."

"Is that how you broke your wrist when you were eight?"

"Guilty. Didn't I tell you that?"

"No. You were covering up for your brothers. I was so sure they'd goaded you to do something that I insisted that your father had to reprimand them. He took them all to the woodshed and talked to them about how their sister would grow up to be a lady, so they should stop teaching you how to be a hellion."

Naomi snickered. "Didn't do much good, did it?"

Her mother sighed. "Alas, no. But at least we tried."

"And no long-term harm done, right?"

"No? Then why are two of your brothers married, and you don't even date anyone long enough to introduce them to your family?"

Naomi rolled her eyes. "Mom! I'm not even thirty yet! Besides, I'm rich and famous, remember? I could have my pick of men if I was willing to support them. But I'm not. I'm a picky woman. But I know what I like. When I meet him, and we both feel the same way, I'll be sure to bring him home for dinner."

"Who will you bring home for dinner? Have you met a man?"

They both looked up as Gramma walked toward them from the main trail.

"*Et tu*, Gramma?" Naomi leaned backward dramatically, with the back of her hand over her forehead as she sighed deeply.

Her grandmother snickered as she approached them. "I heard voices, so I figured it would be my girls. No one else comes out here anymore."

"I could tell by the peeling paint supplemented by the bird crap on the table." Marie made a wry face as she got up, making a big deal out of brushing her hands off on her jeans.

"And the long grass around here, like no one ever mows here anymore. But the swings are still fun."

"Yes, you always did like the swings more than anything else here." Gramma pursed her lips as if reluctant to say anymore. Then her face brightened into a smile. "Let's go up and make a big jar of sun tea. We can have a picnic on the lawn and enjoy the sunshine."

"I thought you were going to nap, Gramma," Naomi reminded her.

"I probably will. But after we get some fresh air and some sunshine."

They had a light meal of a ham, veggie, and cheesy grits casserole, along with some cut-up melon and peanut butter cookies. Soon after that, Gramma excused herself to go inside for a nap.

Naomi and her mom both stayed out enjoying the sunshine, the sounds of the birds, and the warm breezes. They both started out reading. But without being aware of it, both soon drifted off into a light snooze, totally relaxed and in the best of company.

CHAPTER NINE

The door banged open when Gramma stepped out onto the porch, then nudged each of them with her foot. "Wake up, sleepy heads. I'm heading up to the big house now to get the dinner going. Remember, you're both expected for dinner, so since serving starts at five, you should plan to be up there about four-thirty."

Naomi sat up with a yawn. "Do we have to dress up?"

Her mother, stretching beside her, grinned. "Of course we do, sweetie. We're the guests. And Sunday supper is more formal than a weekday dinner."

"I don't know if I brought anything that will qualify as dressed-up."

"Then we'd best get into the house and compare what we brought. I'm sure we can both come up with something to make ourselves presentable. Don't want to make it seem like we don't know how to behave in polite company, right? Like we weren't brought up with manners?"

Gramma, who was just starting along the path, turned back with a grin. "We all know better, of course. But your mom's right, Delu. No one expects you to enjoy yourself. You're just there because you were asked to be. And soon, we'll all be back here, so we can compare notes while we relax."

"Then can we open that bottle of wine I brought?"

Naomi turned to her mother. "You brought one, too?"

Gramma laughed. "Yes, you two. We can open one. Or maybe we'll go wild and drink both of them. I'll see you later." She turned back to the path.

By picking from each other's suitcase, and matching accessory items like scarves, Naomi and her mother were soon suitably attired for the more formal Sunday supper up at the big house.

"Just in time, too," Naomi said with a grin. "It's almost four-thirty, Mom. We'd better shake a leg."

With one last glance at herself in the mirror, her mom nodded, and they locked up the cottage to begin walking up to supper.

When the front door was opened, the old servant smiled happily at those he was admitting into the house. "Why, Miss Marie! And your lovely daughter, too? Miss Naomi. You're a sight for sore eyes, both of you." He bowed to both of them.

"Thank you, Jim." Marie smiled at him. "It's been so long I was afraid you wouldn't recognize us."

He shook his head. "Your beauty will never fade, Miss Marie. But Miss Naomi has gotten so tall! I think the last time I saw you, you were a teenager."

"Yup. Probably the same age Hannah was when she was my babysitter, huh?"

His eyebrows rose up. He furtively glanced around before speaking in a quiet tone. "They don't mention her name aloud anymore. It distresses the mistress too much."

"Thanks for the warning, Jim." Naomi nodded at him.

He showed them into the dining room, where there was a small crowd of people milling around, drinks in hand, as the late afternoon sunshine made the room glow, and the light breeze gently wafted in through the open French Doors.

An older woman smiled when she saw them and rushed over to greet them. "Marie! It's been too long." She clasped both of Marie's hands in hers before pulling her closer to air-kiss both of her cheeks.

"So good to see you again, Miss Elizabeth," Marie replied.

"Oh please, you're an adult now, Marie. You must call me Elizabeth. And this must be your lovely daughter Naomi? My, you've grown into a beautiful young woman, my dear."

She reached over to clasp both of Naomi's hands also, repeating the both-cheeks-air-kisses. "I was so excited when Giselle explained *why* she wanted last night's dinner off. Of course we were glad to give her a night off to spend with her family. And we were even more pleased when she assured us that you'd come to share our Sunday supper with us." She waved a hand around vaguely at the other people in the room. "Of course, we had to invite a few people to meet you. After all, it's not every day that you get to meet a best-selling author." She gave a special smile to Naomi, who grinned back at her.

"Thanks for your hospitality in inviting us, Miss Elizabeth. But that's not the kind of greeting I usually get as an author."

"No?" An older man joined them, bowing to both of his guests before lightly resting his hand on his wife's shoulder. "Marie, Naomi, so delightful to have you both joining us tonight." The pleasantries given, he turned to Naomi to question her. "How are you usually greeted?"

"Well, when I tell people I'm a published author, most are really interested. *What do you write,* is usually their first question. But when I say that I write romance books, often they get a look on their face like they just stepped into some dog poo. *Oh, I don't know anyone who reads that kind of stuff.*"

A woman who appeared to be older than Naomi but younger than her mother overheard and giggled. "Then they're lying. *Everyone* I know has heard of the famous Delu Morris, who writes both *The Highlander* series and the *Spies in the Skies* series. Your books are best-sellers! They're just being ridiculous."

Naomi nodded. "But their whole idea is to be dismissive. Lots of people don't have much respect for fiction novels in general. Add in that my stories involve strong females who have romances and own their sexuality . . . and that they're written by a woman, for women to read? That just opens up a whole can of misogyny disguised as literary criticism."

The woman put her arm around Elizabeth's waist, leaning her head toward her in a quick embrace. "Thanks for inviting her to supper, Mom. I'm so excited to actually meet one of my favorite authors! In fact"—she leaned closer to Naomi—"I knew you were going to be here, so I brought some of my books from home. You don't mind signing them for me, do you?"

Naomi glanced at her mother and was amused by the disapproval on her face. She turned to the other woman. "No, of course I don't mind. But you'll have to give me a name to write on the books."

The older man spoke quickly. "Oh, how rude we've been. Naomi, may I present my daughter-in-law, Michelle, who's married to our younger son, Harold."

A man who was across the room getting another drink turned around as his name was mentioned to wave at Naomi. "That's me. Hello, Naomi. You've kept my wife up late many nights, reading *just-one-more-chapter* of your books. So I don't have to have read them to know you're a good writer. I'm pleased to meet you."

Michelle impulsively leaned closer to hug Naomi. "And I'm thrilled to meet you, Naomi."

Harold walked over, accompanied by another man who appeared to be close in age to him. "And may I present our neighbor, and one of my oldest friends, since we grew up together, Daniel Worthington. His parents own the estate just west of ours."

Not sure of what to do, Naomi held her hand out to the tall man with thinning blond hair.

He bowed, taking her hand and kissing the back of it. "I'm pleased to meet you, *famous author Naomi*. I'm embarrassed to say I've never heard of you, but then as you just pointed out, men aren't usually among your readership. However, for such a beautiful woman, I may need to make an exception."

Naomi looked over to see her mother's face was stern as she shook her head almost imperceptibly.

Naomi pulled her hand back. There was an awkward silence for a heartbeat.

Elizabeth looked distressed. "Oh my, we've barely introduced ourselves to you, but, as yet, no one has offered you a drink. What can my husband get for you, my dears?"

Marie spoke up. "A glass of white wine would be wonderful."

Naomi nodded. "For me, too, also, please."

"Coming right up," the older gentleman said, walking back to the liquor area.

"I don't drink much myself," Elizabeth confided, leaning closer to her guests. "But I do like a glass of wine with dinner. I hope chardonnay is fine with you two?"

"Oh yes, thank you," Marie replied.

Marie and Naomi had barely gotten their glasses when a dinner bell was clearly heard being rung.

"It's time for us to be seated, my dears." The older man, who was the host of the supper, waved toward the table.

Elizabeth looked around frowning. "Oh no! Seven is such an unlucky number for supper. Where on earth is Henry?"

A bald man still tying his tie appeared in the doorway. "Here, Mother." He rapidly moved over to kiss his mother on the cheek. "I'm sorry," he announced to everyone in general, "But when I'm riding Lightning, my favorite horse, I often lose track of time. I'm just lucky I glanced at my watch in time to be here for supper."

Everyone moved over to the table. There were no place settings, so Naomi waited to see if the hosts would have any preference. She was amused to feel her hand grabbed as a voice spoke into her ear.

"I want to sit next to you. I want to hear all about any new books you might have planned for that sexy hunk Laird Duncan." Michelle's eyes sparkled as she grinned.

Naomi saw her mother sitting down next to Elizabeth, and she patted the chair next to her. Naomi drifted over to sit down, and Michelle promptly sat next to her on the other side. Once everyone was seated, Naomi glanced around the table. She was disconcerted to see that the neighbor, Daniel, was across from her, regarding her with a steady stare as if trying to memorize her face. *Wow! Not like that's going to make for an uncomfortable dining experience or anything. Quit staring, you creep!*

Mr. Reynolds proposed a toast to his special guests, and everyone raised their glasses to join him in welcoming Marie and Naomi to their gathering. Shortly after that, he led them in saying grace before supper was served.

Naomi decided that she'd try to avoid looking directly at the man across from her. Since her mother and Elizabeth were chatting easily, they included her in much of their conversation. And when she wasn't participating in their topics, Michelle monopolized her, trying to pry any advanced knowledge of *works-in-progress* so she could impress her reading club.

Supper showed off some of her grandmother's specialties. There was a French onion soup to begin with, followed by a tiny dab of lemon sorbet to cleanse everyone's palate. There was a wild greens salad, then another dab of sorbet. The entree was a ham that had been basted with apricot preserves as it baked, which was served along with a brie and shallots compote served with cornbread toast points. Asparagus had been grilled with vinegarette dressing, and corn was mixed with red and green sweet peppers.

Once everyone had eaten their fill, coffee was served to those who requested it. Harold and Daniel revisited the bar area to refill their glasses with the amber liquor they'd been drinking.

Soon small slivers of pecan pie were delivered to everyone, with multiple bowls of freshly whipped cream placed around the table.

"Oh, I never put whipped cream on my pie," Michelle announced. "A girl's gotta watch her figure, even when she's already got a man." She smiled at her husband sitting across from her.

He winked at her. "I appreciate that, darling. Though I hope you won't mind if I indulge myself?"

She blew him an air-kiss.

Naomi shrugged. "I love Gramma's pies . . . any kind. And I'm not about to waste good whipped cream by not having any of it. So please pass it to me when you're done with it." She addressed that to Daniel.

He arched an eyebrow at her. "You must have a high metabolism to be able to eat so heartily yet maintain such a lovely figure."

That's not weird or anything, is it? God, I hope you don't consider that to be flirting with me! Ew! Naomi gave him a weak smile before applying her full attention to the whipped cream.

Luckily Harold broke the silence this time by poking his friend in the ribs. "Down, boy. She's too young for you."

Daniel glanced at his friend, then returned to staring at Naomi. "Why? Just because she was only a toddler when I was a teenager, hanging around your house all of the time? I know Hannah was her babysitter, but I never was."

There was a quick gasp from Elizabeth.

This time the silence was immediate and drawn out.

Marie leaned over to pat Elizabeth's shaking hand. "Would you like to get some air, Elizabeth? We can take our pie out onto the veranda and enjoy the beginning of the sunset."

"Yes, please," Elizabeth murmured quietly.

They got up to move.

All of the men rose, then sat back down as they exited the room.

"What possessed you to do that?" Harold hissed at Daniel. "You know we don't mention her name in front of Mom. It distresses her too much."

Daniel shrugged. "She's been gone a long time. I haven't been to supper here for quite a while. I guess I didn't realize it was still such a touchy subject."

"And you won't be here again for supper anytime soon," Mr. Reynolds announced, his disapproval heavy in his voice. "Honestly, I thought your parents raised you better."

Daniel took a long sip from his glass. "I'm sorry if I offended your wife, Mr. Henry. But we all remember her, right? Not talking about her isn't going to bring her back. And not talking about her makes it seem like she never was. That can't be right."

"Never-the-less, we don't mention her name in front of my wife," the senior Henry Reynolds said sternly. He turned to Naomi. "I'm very sorry, my dear. It's a painful episode in our family, and some people don't exercise the sense they were born with." He glared at Daniel.

"I thought the psycho-analysis she had done years ago would have helped her to cope." Daniel was obviously oblivious to the *faux pas* he'd made.

Mr. Reynolds turned to Naomi again. "I'm sorry you have to be party to this discussion, Naomi. If you'd rather join your mother and my dear wife out on the veranda?"

Naomi shrugged. "Why? All families have their issues. Mine usually involves my gay brother and his partner *du jour*. Besides, I'm seeing an analyst of sorts myself now."

Michelle raised both eyebrows. "You? Whatever for? You're rich, famous, and a best-selling author. Why on earth do you need to be analyzed?"

"It's nothing really major. Just some recent panic attacks

and some anxiety issues. But things like that can fester if you don't deal with them. The guy I'm going to is a pioneer in a new kind of therapy. He uses a machine to enter your dreams with you, so he can help you revisit any memories that might be causing you trouble."

"Dream-therapy? I've heard of that." The younger Henry leaned forward, more interested. "I've got a degree in psychology. I work at a local high school as a counselor. But I've read about the doctor I think you're talking about. Dr. Alan Banning, who's doing his research at Virginia Tech, right?"

Naomi nodded. "Yes. I've only seen him a few times. So far, we haven't discovered anything that might indicate why hearing loud arguments gives me panic attacks. But he assures me we'll find the cause by . . . how did he explain it . . . *pulling up the shade* my subconscious drew down to protect me from whatever memory is so distressing to me. I'm just hoping he can find it. It's been hampering my writing." She gave an apologetic grin to Michelle. "That's why I've been unable to give you any insider scoop. I'm not really working on anything right now."

Naomi was dismayed to notice with her peripheral vision that Daniel still seemed to be studying her closely. She was uncomfortable with his scrutiny, so she concentrated on chatting about her books with Michelle.

They both looked up when the men excused themselves to drift off to the study for post-prandial brandy and cigars.

Michelle made a face, rolling her eyes. "I hate when he has a cigar! I make him brush his teeth before he can kiss me. They smell so nasty."

Naomi shrugged. "I've never smoked anything, so I agree with you." She changed the subject. "Do you live nearby?"

Michelle nodded. "Oh yes. We live just outside of town, in a newer Mc-mansion with a pretty sizable yard. We're trying to get pregnant. We both want to have at least a couple of kids, and I want them to have room to play. Harold grew up here with the grounds to roam around on. But I want a swing set and sandbox and room for the kids to learn how to play soccer."

Naomi smiled. "Did you play in school?"

Michelle nodded vigorously. "All through my childhood. When I was a senior, I was on the high school team that made state champions." She looked around furtively. "No one else is around now. Do you want me to bring in my bag of books for you to autograph?"

Naomi shrugged. "Your car can't be that far away, right? I think we could both use the exercise walking out there. That way, there won't be any chance of you forgetting them here."

"Are you kidding? Once they're autographed, they'll become my most treasured possessions. But if that's okay with you, then let's go before anyone else tries to engage us in conversation."

"Then after that, we should join Mom and your mother-in-law out on the veranda. It's a nice evening, and we can watch the sunset with them."

"That's a great idea. Let's go."

The group broke up soon after the sunset, which was enjoyed by all of them out on the veranda. Elizabeth was the first to announce that she was tired and wanted to head up to her room.

"And we'll be headed back to my mother's cottage," Marie explained. "We've only got one more night to spend with her. Thanks for having us to supper tonight. We enjoyed your hospitality."

Naomi nodded. "Yes, Miss Elizabeth, your home is beautiful. Thank you for welcoming me into it."

Elizabeth leaned close to air-kiss Naomi again on both cheeks. "My dear, you're always welcome in my home."

She turned to take Marie's hand and squeezed it. "It was lovely to see you again, Marie. And to get a chance to speak with your beautiful daughter. She's grown into such a polished, well-spoken young woman. I'm sure she brings much joy into your life . . ." Her voice ended with a small sob that she tried to hide.

Marie gave her a quick hug. "She does, Elizabeth. And thank you for sharing your home with us."

Naomi and her mother walked out to the foyer, accompanied by Michelle and Harold.

"Thanks again for autographing my books, Naomi. And I'll be sure to register as part of your *street-team* on your website so I can get any insider info you share with your fans."

Harold chuckled. "Oh? You know, if I didn't know better, I might be offended that I'm not supplying your life with enough romance, and that's why you enjoy her books so much."

Michelle reached up to pat his cheek. "It's not that, darling. But we're already married. I do so enjoy experiencing that *newly-fallen-in-love feeling*, along with the agony of wondering if the feeling is returned and the ecstasy of discovering it is. Plus, her heroes are so darned hot!"

He rolled his eyes. "Fine. As long as they keep you too happy to even think about leaving me."

"Oh, I'd never do that. I've invested too much time in you already. Besides, we're trying to get pregnant, remember? Reading her books keeps *me in the mood*, all the time."

He snorted with laughter, trying to cover up his blush. "Fine."

Naomi grinned. "Good night, you two. It was so nice meeting you."

She and Marie thanked the butler, who held the door open for them again as they left.

Later, when they were joined in the cottage by Giselle, Marie opened her bottle of wine first, and they sipped it while they sat in the comfortable living room discussing their opinions on how the dinner had gone.

After they had complimented Giselle on her excellent cooking, Naomi voiced the question that had been bothering her. "Why don't they mention the name of the girl who used to babysit for me? She was the only daughter of the house, right? With two older brothers?"

Giselle and Marie exchanged quick glances.

"What?" Naomi pressed.

Giselle took a deep breath before she spoke. "It happened a long time ago, honey. Hannah was a delightful young lady. Despite having only brothers, she was well-mannered and very ladylike. She took after her mother."

"Not like some females we know," Marie added in a low voice, grinning at her daughter.

"Mom! Stop. I'm not as much of a tomboy as I used to be. And I think I proved tonight that I do know how to be well-mannered. Even if I don't practice my skills much."

Marie blew her a kiss, nodding.

Giselle smiled. "All of the serving girls told me what a well-brought-up young lady I have as a granddaughter."

Marie snickered. "They were just hoping for a chance at any leftover pecan pie, Mom!"

Naomi rolled her eyes at her mother before turning to her grandmother. "Go on, please, Gramma."

"She was seventeen that first summer when you came to stay with me. She had loved playing with dolls as a child, so when you appeared, she decided that she wanted to be your babysitter. Since you were so young, I'd been wondering how I would keep you entertained when I had to work. Her offer to take you to the playground, or to let you play with some of her dolls from when she was young, was a godsend. You seemed to enjoy your time with her, and frequently you were so tired after playing with her all day that you'd fall asleep soon after I gave you your nightly bath. You'd be covered with dirt and sand from playing all kinds of games with her. She taught you how to jump rope using the rhymes and chants that girls amuse themselves with. She even enlisted Henry and Harold to spin the ropes so she could try to teach you how to jump double-Dutch. But you were too young for that."

Naomi shook her head. "I don't remember any of that."

Marie patted the back of her hand. "No one expects you to, honey. You were just a toddler."

"Yeah. I don't even remember my grade school days much. Forget about kindergarten. And this was when I was, what, like three, four?"

Marie nodded. "Yes. I went back to work full-time at the start of summer when you were three, so being able to send you here was a godsend for me. And you spent time here during the school year also."

"So what happened to her that her own mother won't let her name be mentioned in front of her?"

Giselle and Marie exchanged a look with pursed lips.

Giselle shrugged. "No one really knows what happened to her or how. We only know the aftermath. It seems that Hannah had snuck out of the house after she was supposed to be in bed. She was seventeen, and you know how teenagers are."

Marie lifted an eyebrow and poked her daughter. "Yes, Mom. I know what teenage girls are like. Hell on wheels!"

Naomi stuck her tongue out at her mom. "Go on, Gramma."

"No one realized she wasn't in the house until the morning when the maid went in to wake her up because she was late for breakfast. She wasn't in her room, nor was there a note or any indication as to where she'd gone. But her bed hadn't been slept in.

"Meanwhile, I'd had a sleepless night because I was woken up by a branch hitting my window, and for some reason, I went to check on you. You weren't in your bed. I was sure you must have snuck out, but I had no idea when. I went out and spent some time looking for you, calling your name, and using my flashlight. I yelled so loudly that I woke up Jim calling for you near his cabin. He came out onto his porch and asked me what was wrong, and when I told him, he grabbed his flashlight to join me in looking for you."

Naomi patted her grandmother's hand because it was trembling. "Obviously, you found me. And it was a long time ago, Gramma."

"Yes, but I still remember how worried I was. Jim and I were both searching all of the areas we knew you played in with Hannah. When we got to the playground, I heard a small sound. I ran over to the bushes and found you there crying. You told me that you'd gone there to play with Hannah, but she wasn't there, and you were scared being alone at night, so you hid under the nearby bushes. Then you had a bad dream, but you cried yourself back to sleep. Our shouting had woken you up again. I pulled you into my arms, and you held on for dear life with a strength I didn't realize you had. Jim walked us back to my place, and I gave you some hot cocoa, then put you back to bed."

"But what about Hannah?"

Giselle sighed. "The family notified the police once they discovered her missing. Her body was discovered two days later, in a shallow grave near the high school football field."

Naomi swallowed. "They found the killer, right?"

Giselle shook her head. "No. There was an investigation, and any boys she'd ever been seen with were questioned. But no one was ever charged in her rape and murder."

Naomi gulped. "Rape?"

Giselle nodded. "Yes. Someone had violated her and strangled her. It almost killed Miss Elizabeth when she learned what had happened. Mr. Henry was the one who went to identify the body at the morgue. Neither of them have ever been the same since then."

"And Miss Elizabeth went to an analyst to try to recover from her shock, right?"

Giselle nodded. "Yes, sweetie. She wasn't sleeping or eating, and it was hard for anyone to get her interested in staying alive. Her husband and sons were worried they'd lose her, too. So she spent some time staying in a place, being medicated. Then when she came home, she continued to do outpatient visits for years. She had been a strong, vibrant woman. Losing her daughter like that crushed her into the thin, fragile woman she is now."

Naomi sat back, shaking her head. "Wow. Just . . . wow. I had no idea. No wonder they don't mention her daughter's name in front of her."

Marie shook her head. "That ignorant twit from the next estate has to have known not to say her name, but he did anyway. I had to get her out of the room before she broke down in tears."

Giselle's eyebrows rose. "Daniel said her name in front of Miss Elizabeth?"

The other two women nodded.

Giselle's eyes flashed with anger. "Well, it will be a cold day in hell before he's invited over to the house again. And even then, it won't be for Sunday supper. Honestly, he comes from a good family. But he's always been headstrong and rebellious."

"I guess there's one in every family, right?" Naomi's eyes sparkled.

Her mother leaned forward. "Oh? To whom are you referring, my dear? You, my unmarried author daughter who travels all over the globe promoting her smutty books? Or her gay brother who expects his family to accept his boyfriends, even though most don't last long enough for us to remember their names?"

"Mom, puh-leeze! I've always told you I won't bring a man home until I'm confident that he's *the one*. I don't think I've met him yet." Almost as an afterthought, she added quietly, "Or if I have, nothing has progressed to that level."

Giselle was the one to lean forward this time. "Oh? A new man in your life? Come on, girl. Spill to your gramma! Inquiring minds want details."

Naomi laughed. "There's nothing much to tell you, really. The grad student who works with my dreams doctor is a very cute Scotsman. In fact, the first time I walked into the office, he was wearing a kilt! His hair is so dark it looks black. A real contrast with his very pale skin, and piercing blue eyes. He looks like I've always imagined my Laird Duncan would look."

"Hmm, wears a kilt, does he?" Marie smirked at her daughter. "Does he wear it *authentic style*?"

Naomi could feel her skin heat up with her blush. "Mom! I have no idea what he does or doesn't wear under his kilt! I've only seen him in the office when I'm there for my appointments."

Both older women regarded her silently — and expectantly.

"Well, okay. And when you called me on Friday afternoon to suggest we come out here, we were having coffee together in the student center."

"Coffee, huh?"

"Mom! Stop it! He was afraid to even talk to me because he's a part of my therapy team, and he doesn't want to lose his job because he's fraternizing with a client. Even though I'm not *his* client, but the doctor's."

Marie sighed. "This is all because we took that trip to

Scotland when you were at such an impressionable age, isn't it? Your first books were about a hot-blooded man in a kilt. I wonder if this young man can live up to your expectations."

Giselle smiled. "I can remember another young woman who never brought any boys home to meet her family. Then suddenly, one day, she introduced one to us all, and we realized we had no say in her decision. Because apparently, she'd gone and fallen for him, and once her mind was made up, there was no talking to her about moderation or taking things slowly. Was there?" She smirked at her daughter.

"Mom! Not in front of Naomi!"

"What? Mom is scandalized? Please, do go on, Gramma dear. Didn't Dad make a good impression on the family? He's usually good with people."

"Yes. But we didn't want to like him. He was a gangly, middle-class white boy with blond cowlicks sticking up all over his head. It was obvious he was head-over-heels in love with our Marie, but we had hoped for a better match for her."

"Better?"

Marie bowed to the inevitable. "Your father wasn't rich back then. In fact, he was fairly poor compared to some I'd dated before him. But he had ambition, and I was so in love with him that I believed he'd achieve all of his glorious plans."

"And did he?"

Marie's lips quirked upward at the corners. "As a matter of fact, yes, he did. Most of them, anyway. And we've never wanted for anything, have we?"

Giselle nodded. "True, he's been a good provider. And he treats my baby girl right, so I can't complain. Not that it would ever do any good anyway."

Marie huffed. "Well, Mom, I can remember Gramma talking about how she had higher ambitions for you. She wanted you to go to college, not culinary school. And when you met a boy there who was also planning to be a chef, you brought him home to announce you were engaged."

Naomi smiled while opening the second bottle of wine. "This is getting good. Did I ever meet Great-Gramma?" She poured more wine into all three not-surprisingly empty glasses.

The laughter and conversation lasted long into the night. Getting tipsy and sharing tasty snacks allowed for much teasing, as well as sharing of family stories. When Giselle finally yawned and leaned back, closing her eyes, Marie and Naomi helped her into her room and into her bed. And because they had a drive tomorrow to get back to their lives, they went to bed at the same time.

CHAPTER TEN

Naomi walked quickly down the hall, heading for her therapy appointment. She glanced at her watch as she reached for the door handle. *Only five minutes late. I hope they're not all setup and sitting around waiting for me.*

She was a little out of breath as she entered the waiting room. She sat down and picked up a magazine, hoping that since the receptionist was on the phone, she wouldn't notice that the next client was a tad late.

Maggie nodded, saying, "Well, it can't be helped. Please get him out the door as quickly as possible."

She looked over to Naomi and smiled. "I'm sorry, Naomi, but your appointment is going to be a bit delayed. Seems that Will scheduled himself a dentist appointment for during his lunch break, and they're running a bit behind. So he's not back yet. You're welcome to wait, or I can reschedule your appointment."

Naomi returned her smile. "Oh, that's fine. I'll wait."

The inner door opened, and Dr. Banning waved to Naomi. "That won't be necessary, my dear. I've gotten one of the other grad students in our department to stop by. He's familiar with the machine and has observed my sessions a few times, so he knows the procedure. This way we're not dependent on Will's return. Please, come in."

The grad student was tuning the equipment when Naomi entered the room. He looked up with a smile. "My name is Ishan Patel. I'm pleased to meet you, Miss Morrison."

Naomi smiled back at him. "Hi, Ishan."

Dr. Banning bustled over to begin getting her ready for her relaxation exercises. He turned to Ishan. "You're sure you've got all of the connections settled and the machine is working?"

"It does appear to be, sir. I've done everything you told me to, and the green light indicates that it's ready for use."

"I'll apply the electrodes to Naomi while you monitor the machine."

After he'd taken care of Naomi, the doctor sat on his bench to apply his own electrodes. Ishan held the scented oil under Naomi's nose for some deep breathing, then she began to chant with the doctor to settle herself into her dream state.

She had just drifted off when she was suddenly awoken by the doctor growling at his substitute assistant.

"What do you mean you can't make it work? Everything was working all morning. Nothing has changed other than you don't know what you're doing, that's all." He rose from his bench, pushing the younger man out of the way as he adjusted the connections and dials on the machine.

"You see? I told you it's all working correctly. I'm not doing anything wrong."

The doctor's voice was heavy with sarcasm. "Well, you must not be doing everything right, or I'd be walking with her in her dreams already. But I'm not, so obviously something is not right. The only thing I can see is operator error."

The younger man drew himself up as if to argue when the door swung open, and a breathless Will strode into the room.

"Sorry te be late. Ah'd an emergency toothache. Otherwise, Ah'd not have agreed to an appointment during practice hours. But Ah'm here now."

Doctor Banning sniffed at him. "I hope your mind is clearer than your speaking right now."

"Sorry. *Novocaine.* Ah can assure you, Ah'm ready and able to work, Doctor."

Ishan appeared to be slinking toward the door when Doctor Banning spoke loudly. "Where do you think you're going, young man? You need to stay here to watch carefully. Maybe you can figure out what you were doing wrong. I should have another assistant trained, just in case this kind of thing ever happens again."

Will objected. "Ah can assure ye that it willnae."

"Then let us please get on with our current appointment. I'm sure Naomi doesn't plan on spending her entire afternoon with us." With a dismissive sniff, he returned to his bench and lay back.

Naomi was still lying down but smiled at Will when he came to hold the scented oil vial under her nose. "I'm glad you're back," she whispered.

He startled, then grinned at her. He acknowledged her with a nod before turning to go back to his place at the machinery.

Doctor Banning led Naomi in chanting, and almost instantly, she was back in school. She looked around, realizing by the hairstyles, the clothing, and the surroundings, that she was in her high school. Memories flew by in a blur, as her thoroughly ordinary experiences presented themselves, with no trauma of any kind. Even her middle school years were spent enjoying being in the pampered environment of a private school where the teachers excelled at teaching their students manners, as well as academics.

One year bled back into another until she was momentarily taken aback when she looked down and realized that her breasts were gone—but since her best friend was next to her talking animatedly, she stole a glance at her bestie and saw that she also was flat-chested. And judging by who her current best friend was, she realized that she was in fifth grade.

Doctor Banning helped her sift through some memories, each time moving her back to a younger age. She never felt as if anything she was experiencing was important. At any rate, there was never an incident in which others were arguing close to her. If anything, seeing her memories so openly reminded her of what a happy childhood she'd had. They were in her mind for longer than they had been on other appointments, so when she was awoken by the doctor speaking loudly to her, she was momentarily disoriented.

"Oh! I'm back being adult-me now?"

"Yes, Naomi. But I fear we're still no closer to an answer for you."

"Maybe it's not anything that ever happened to me. Maybe it's just anxiety for some other reason? Or I'm secretly stressing over not being able to come up with new ideas to write?"

Doctor Banning regarded her over the top of his glasses as he sat at his desk typing notes into his laptop. "Or maybe this is not the most efficacious therapy for you. There are other methods that you might find your answers with."

Naomi sighed. "I guess."

"But I'm not ready to give up just yet, my dear. On Friday, we'll delve even further back into your memories. We'll start where we left off, with your earliest grade-school classes, then go back to preschool."

"I didn't go to preschool."

"No? Then where did you spend your time before you were old enough for school?"

"Mostly at my grandmother's cottage on the Reynolds estate near Lynchburg."

"Oh? So, it wasn't just your summers that you spent there?"

"No. Mom was home with me until I was three. Then she went back to working full-time. That's when I started spending weeks, even months at a time with Gramma. My brothers were all older and had friends they could hang out with. They'd only come for short stays of a week or so, every so often."

"Well, that's when we'll be aiming for on Friday. If we don't find any answers there, I'm afraid I will have to give you a referral to a colleague of mine who might be able to offer a different way to approach your problem."

"Thanks, Doctor Alan." She nodded at him, then turned to smile at Will. "And thanks, Will, for showing up when you did. Whatever magic touch you have, it worked."

He gave her a lop-sided smile, rubbing at his jaw on the side that was obviously still numb from the *Novocain*.

Naomi turned and left the office, closing the door behind her.

CHAPTER ELEVEN

After spending yet another few hours trying unsuccessfully to get *in the groove* writing again, Naomi stood up, clicking her laptop closed.

Maybe I was more right than I thought when I told the doctor it might be stress anxiety over my muse having deserted me. Maybe I've burned out already. I'm a has-been before thirty. Wouldn't that be a bummer!

Thoroughly depressed by that thought, she glanced out of the window. *It's a gorgeous day out there. The late afternoon sunshine looks golden, and the trees are all in bloom. Maybe a nice long walk is just what I need right now to clear my head.*

She put her laptop into her carrying case and slung it over her shoulder. *I'll walk for a while, then stop and see if I'm inspired to write about anything.* Satisfied that she had a plan of action to implement, she closed her apartment door, locked it, and headed out to enjoy the warm weather with no destination in mind other than a chance to soak up the beauty of nature to soothe her soul.

A short time later, she realized she'd unconsciously headed back to campus and was very near to the coffee shop she'd met Will at on Friday. *It's a warm afternoon. I think a frozen coffee would be a perfect way to cool off.*

After she had her drink, she looked around the indoor seating hopefully but didn't see anyone she recognized. *Ah, who am I kidding? I was hoping to see that sexy Scotsman.* With a sigh, she headed for the outdoor seating. Not seeing him there either, she grabbed a small table and opened up her laptop.

She was still scrolling through emails when she glanced up from taking a sip from her drink in time to see Will walking out of the shop but heading off to the side. Decisively she clicked her laptop closed again and hurried over to catch up with him. She didn't call out his name because she remembered how hesitant he was about being seen in public with her.

It didn't take her long to catch up to him. As she neared him from behind, she spoke quietly. "Hi, Will. Heading out to enjoy the sunshine?"

He startled, then turned. When he saw her, a slow smile crept across his lips.

Those sexy lips I want to kiss! She chided her inner self. *Down, girl!*

"Ah didnae expect to be seein' you again today," he began.

She walked next to him, matching his long stride. "Really? I confess that I was hoping to see you again. There's something I want to ask you about."

One eyebrow rose. "There is? Ah'm headin' towards the pond."

Seeing her puzzled look, he explained. "There's a wee pond where some grad students are wont te toss a line in to see if any fish'll bite. Ah dinnae have a pole, so Ah just hike on the trails that run through the trees there."

"The *Novocain* must be wearing off, since you're a lot easier to understand again."

He smiled. "Ah've been making dentists wealthy mah whole life. Folks from the British Isles are notorious fer havin' bad teeth. If Ah hadnae been in such pain, Ah'd have waited. But Ah had a tooth that demanded work."

She studied his mouth. "Ah, I see. But there really *is* something I want to ask you. Are there any benches where we can sit and talk?"

His eyes widened as they met hers. "Ah still cannae be seen with ye. Yer still a patient o' mine."

Naomi smiled. "Then let's hope there's a bench that's set back in the woods so we can have some privacy while we talk."

Privacy? Will's thoughts whirled around in his head. Ah'd love to get ye in a private place, lassie. Ah need to discover if yer lips are as tasty as they look. He felt his cock thicken with interest as some of the fantasies he'd entertained himself with involving her rushed through his head. *But that has to wait until yer therapy is over. After that, there'll be nae stoppin' me.* He glanced at her and realized that her face looked serious. *But ye seem genuinely concerned aboot sommat. Fine. Talking is good — as long as Ah kin keep mah hands to mahsel.*

Naomi burbled happily when they started on the main trail. "This is lovely! How did I not know this was here? It's in the middle of Blacksburg and in the middle of campus, but it feels so remote . . . like an oasis of nature surviving in the middle of a center of technology. Way cool!" She pointed to people tossing lines into the pond before sitting on folding chairs to watch their bobbers. "Does anyone ever catch anything?"

Will shrugged. "Ah dinnae ken. But hope springs eternal, especially on such a bonnie day."

They walked in silence for a while until Will took a smaller path off to one side, and they walked deeper into the woods. Eventually, they got to an aging bench.

Naomi smiled. "Oh, look! There's lots of scribblings from over the years of eternal love proclamations. Some even have dates. I'll bet they've all long since graduated and moved on with their lives."

"Ye never know when ye'll meet the love of yer life, do ye?"

Naomi gave him a startled look before she sat down, patting the bench next to her. "Sit, and we can talk while we finish our coffee."

Will sat as far away as he could manage on the small bench.

Seeing his discomfort, Naomi put her laptop in between them, and they both drank their coffees while they listened to the birds and the sounds of insects buzzing all around them.

Naomi broke the silence. "Will, why didn't the machinery work for Ishan? I watched him, and he did everything that you always do. It should have worked, but it didn't. Really pissed off Doctor Alan, too."

Will thought about his words before he spoke. "Ah dinnae know, lassie. What do *you* think?"

She gazed off into the woods. "This might sound silly, but I think there's something special that *you* do that Ishan didn't know how to do. Or maybe something he's *not able* to do."

He spoke quietly. "What makes ye say that?"

She turned to look into his eyes. "I've seen you in my dreams."

He felt himself blush. "Ah dinnae know what to say . . ."

She shook her head. "No, not like that. Although there have been a couple like that . . . involving you."

His eyes widened before he turned his head away.

"No, look at me, please, Will. Doctor Alan said that *only he* would be with me in my dreams when we're in my memories. But the characters that live in my head, the ones that I write about? One of them told me she's seen you in my memories, also. And once Cammy told me that, I paid more attention to the shadows the next time I was sharing my dreams with the doctor, and she was right. You were also there. How is that possible? You don't have any electrodes attached to you. Yet there you are, silently watching everything that I've been sharing with the doctor." She met Will's gaze.

Will bit his lips, trying to buy himself time. He shifted on the bench, trying to think of how to respond to her.

"I can see that I've made you uncomfortable, Will, and I'm

sorry. But—wait a minute!"

He turned to see a startled look on her face.

"He doesn't know, does he? He has no idea that you're in my memories, also. How can that be possible? What's going on, Will?"

He took a deep breath, slowly letting it out, as he turned to study her face. "Can Ah trust ye, lassie? What Ah have to tell ye is no sommat that can be blethered aboot."

"A secret?"

He nodded.

Naomi raised her head to look directly into his eyes. "Yes, you can trust me, Will Hamilton. I swear that anything you tell me will remain between the two of us." She whispered, "Because I hope we can still see each other once my therapy is over."

Will was lost in the deep brown of her eyes, wanting to stare into them forever. Finally, he stopped struggling with his inner self. He took another deep breath. "Naomi, did ye do any research before ye wrote yer first Laird Duncan book?"

"Research? About what? What Scotland was like when he was alive?"

He nodded. "And the lore of the Celtic folks. The mythology of the islands."

"Some. I mean, I'd picked up a couple of books about the *wee folks* and the stories about when magic ruled in Scotland. I had to have stories for Duncan to refer to, since they'd have been not just stories but *real* to folks back then."

"No just then," Will said softly.

Naomi's eyebrows both rose. "Please continue."

"Ah have a big family back home. We're nae Catholics, so we got teased a lot in school. But Ah have six older brothers." He saw the confusion on Naomi's face.

"Okay. So, you're from a big family. What does that have

to do with anything?"

He looked away from her before turning to face her again. "Mah faither's also from a large family. It's a part of our clan's traditions. He has two younger sisters, as well as six older brothers."

Naomi's eyes grew wide as she thought that through. "What? So, you're the seventh son of a seventh son?"

He nodded. "Aye. It's a special burden to carry. One that no one in recent memory has had to bear. But it's been passed down to me, and Ah have to carry out mah destiny."

Naomi shook her head. "Destiny? Like what?"

"Ah've heard stories ma whole life about what that involves. Old stories, ones that yer never sure if ye should believe 'em or not. But Ah tend to think there's truth in 'em. See, me faither is the head of the Clan Hamilton. Historically, when a clan is insulted in some way, something that goes beyond the pale . . . that insults the magical powers that surrounded the Celts and still linger on in the islands . . . then there are only a few options. One is that the guilty party needs to be tossed off a high cliff into the sea. The other is that a seventh son of a seventh son must curse that person, to clear the air, so's to speak."

"What does this have to do with you?"

"Ah lived a normal life until a few years ago. Ah was aware of my special status, but it wasnae any problem. Then when Ah was thinkin' of where to do mah grad work, Ah was applyin' to lots of universities. Ah've mah bachelor's degree in technology because that's mah main interest. But a counselor contacted me and offered to help me decide which university would be the best choice for me. When Ah met with him, he encouraged me to combine the psychology classes Ah'd taken for my minor with mah technology degree and to apply to the Virginia Technological Institute.

"Ah'd always wanted to experience the states. Ah've

always enjoyed yer accents. And the southern drawl down here is musical and soothing. So Ah applied, and he directly contacted Doctor Banning to suggest that Ah'd be a useful addition to the grad students he had working with him, trying to get his new machinery to work properly. Ah didnae even tell mah folks Ah'd applied because Ah thought it was a long shot. When Ah got the acceptance letter inviting me to join the doctor in his research, Ah was astounded!"

"And here you are?"

"Ach aye. But when Ah first got accepted, Ah tried to contact the counselor who had been so helpful. Mah emails bounced back as undeliverable. Then Ah tried to call him, but the number he'd given me was disconnected. So Ah decided to drop in to tell him of mah good fortune. But there was a female counselor in his office. When Ah asked about him, she told me she'd been in that office for the past five years. Furthermore, she'd never heard of the man I wanted to see."

He stopped to stare into her bewildered eyes. "That was the first time Ah suspected that mah life wasnae goin' to be mine for a wee while. The magic was going to use me for whatever it needed."

Chapter Twelve

"So what is it, exactly, that the magic is going to use you for?" Naomi was intrigued. Her author-mind was already thinking of ways to use this information in a book.

Will shrugged. "Ah dinnae ken, yet. Ah just know it will be sommat that involves the Hamilton name, and it's something so egregious that the wee folk are offended by it. They want to rectify a wrong done to our clan, and they're going to use me to do it. Ah swear, that's all Ah know fer now."

"So that's why *you* can operate the dream machine, but Ishan, who did all of the same things you do, was unable to launch the doctor into my dreams?"

"Aye. Ye see, lassie, when Ah touch the controls, Ah send a wee bit o' magic into them through mah fingertips. And dinnae bother asking *how* Ah do it. Ah dinnae ha'e a clue. It just happens. Ah can feel it pass through mah fingers into the machinery. Then Ah find mysel' in two places at once—holding the controls, and in yer dreams also. Since Ah'm nae supposed to be there, Ah stick to the shadows on the periphery of yer vision. Yer nae supposed to see me there."

Naomi grinned. "I told you, the characters in my head talk to me in my dreams. Cammy, the heroine of my spy books, asked me why there were strangers appearing in my head. I told her about Dr. Alan, but she asked specifically about you. Then the next time, I looked for you and saw you there."

Will leaned his head back, his eyes closed. "Ah. That explains things."

"Not really. I mean, I have voices in my head because my

99

characters live there. They usually only speak to me in dreams. But we can have conversations. And we're useful to each other. They tell me their stories, which is how I write my books. But after writing my books, others read them. That lets them live in other people's heads also. Instead of being stuck in just *my* head, they can move into readers' heads and live there, too. Win-win for all of us. Do the entities in your head talk to you?"

Will shook his head with a shudder. "No, and Ah hope they ne'er do! You've heard of the Seelie and the Unseelie?"

Naomi nodded. "Yes. The Seelie are the good spirits, and the Unseelie are the bad ones, right?"

"It's nae that easy. They're both members of fairy courts, and sometimes they intermingle. But the Seelie are the ones who provide blessings to humans, while the Unseelie are the ones involved with curses. So Ah'm afraid that if a curse is what's required, the beings inside of me must be Unseelie. And the less Ah know aboot them, the better."

"Why? Are you afraid of them? I mean, if they're using you to achieve something, they must find you useful. So, they won't hurt you, right? Just the one you're supposed to find for them?"

Will gazed into her eyes thoughtfully. "Ah sure hope so. Ah dinnae ha'e any way of knowin' what it is Ah'm supposed to do, or who it is Ah'm supposed to connect them with. But knowing that there are fairies with evil intent living in mah heed is unsettlin', to say the least."

Naomi smiled as she put one hand on her laptop and used the free hand to gently pat the side of Will's troubled face. "There, there, Will. You know from history, and from stories, that this isn't the first time a seventh son of a seventh son has been used to work a curse. But those guys survived afterward, right? So, all you have to do is let them do what they need to, and they'll leave you alone, right?"

Will was still staring into her eyes as if seeking reassurance.

Naomi felt her breath hitch as she leaned even closer to him. Their faces were so close it was just a matter of leaning a bit further, and their lips would touch. So she did.

Will leaned into the kiss, also.

Naomi felt like she was playing with fire since Will's lips felt so hot. He drew back slightly to tentatively lick at her lips. She opened her mouth with a breathy sigh and rejoiced as their tongues became acquainted with each other. Her hand moved down to his shoulder, and she leaned even closer to him.

Will's hand moved up to touch her face, then traveled to her hair to massage the back of her scalp and pull her face even closer to his.

Heedless of her laptop, she moved closer to him, hearing a moan come from him as he adjusted himself so that more of their bodies touched.

Naomi felt herself tingling in places she'd been ignoring lately. Her nipples beaded and poked against her bra. She could feel moisture pooling between her thighs as her body began to ready itself for the inevitable joining with the man she'd been lusting after for weeks. Her pulse was quick, and her breathing shallow. And she was ready to strip if he asked her to so they could do what they both wanted so badly to do.

Suddenly Naomi realized how close she was to getting naked in a very public place with the man who was afraid to even be seen with her. She opened her eyes and let out a startled squeak.

"Will, your eyes! What's wrong with your eyes?"

He drew back, looking like he was having trouble pulling himself back from the same brink of passion that she'd been on. "What do ye mean? What's wrong with ma een?"

"There's no blue in them anymore!" She tried not to sound as horrified as she felt.

He stared at her. "What color are they, lassie?"

"Black. There isn't even much white showing at all, and no blue. Just black."

Will stood up quickly, glancing around with terror. "Ah feel them! They're here! They've been spying on us. They realized what we both want and tried to nudge us into acting on our impulses. They want to feel what Ah feel! Ah have to leave now, lassie! And Ah cannae touch ye again. Not while they're still in ma heed!"

"Will, wait!"

But it was no use. Will turned and fled as if the devil was after him.

No, Naomi realized. *The devil isn't behind him. There are many of them, and they're inside his head. No wonder he's so freaked out. I'm used to sharing my head-space with other voices. He's not.*

She got up with a sigh, putting the laptop strap over her shoulder. *Oh, Will, your lips tasted so good. I've been having lustful thoughts about you ever since I saw you in your kilt. I just hope the fairies lead you to do what they need you to do soon so you and I can do what we both want to do without an audience of evil spirits in your head, vicariously enjoying what we're doing.*

She was retracing her steps back to the pond when a sudden thought startled her, and she stopped. *Wait a minute! Does that mean that the characters living in my head get to watch and enjoy when I'm having sex? I never thought of that before!* A slow smile crawled across her face. She'd have to ask Cammy the next time she popped up in a dream. Laird Duncan would be too embarrassed if she asked him. But Cammy would tell her the truth. *She'd better, or I won't write her another exciting adventure with hot, hard men for her to amuse herself with.*

When she got back to her apartment, Naomi plugged her laptop in and opened a blank page. She started typing. When she stopped to find something to drink, she realized she'd been writing for a couple of hours. And there was a new Laird

Duncan story coming to life. She smiled as she opened a bottle of Riesling she'd found in her fridge and poured some into a glass.

She called and placed an order for delivery from the middle eastern cafe a few blocks away and happily envisioned pairing their falafel and hummus with her wine. Then she changed into a pair of comfortable gym shorts and a t-shirt, and got back to her writing.

CHAPTER THIRTEEN

On Friday morning, Naomi was still drinking her morning coffee while she picked out what she was going to wear to her appointment. She almost ignored the phone when it rang, because she didn't want to be late. But she glanced at it and was surprised to see that it was Doctor Banning's office calling.

"Hello?"

"Oh, Miss Morrison, I'm so glad I caught you before you got here. You're not driving or anything, are you?" The secretary sounded anxious.

"No. I haven't left for my appointment yet. Why? Do we have to reschedule?"

"I'm not sure if we should."

Naomi was definitely curious now. "Why? Has something happened?"

"Yes! Doctor Banning was in a car accident yesterday. He was crossing the street to get from here to the parking garage. He was struck by a hit-and-run driver. They rushed him to the nearest ER at Lewis Gale. I can't share any other details right now. I'm sorry."

"Don't be silly! None of this is your fault, or the doctors, either. Please let me know if there's anything that I can do to help. Once he's stabilized and can have visitors, I'd like to check in with him. After all, he's spent so much time in my head I feel like we're friends, not just doctor and patient."

"I will, Miss Morrison. And thank you for being so understanding. I've been calling his other patients, and some

104

haven't been as nice as you."

"Naomi," she gently reminded the woman. "And remember to take care of yourself, Maggie. I'm sure this is a shock for you to deal with. Maybe you should go home early."

"You're so right. I've never known anyone who was in an accident before. Now I'm afraid to walk across the street myself. But it's the only way to get back to my car. Thanks for being so kind. I'll talk to you again soon."

"Bye."

Naomi sat looking at her phone for a while, thinking about what she'd just learned. *What a horrible thing to have happened! I wonder if it's a disgruntled ex-patient who has a grudge against the doctor? Or was it just an accident?* Either way, if she was going to do some more writing today, she should work off some bad vibes at the gym. It was raining, so she couldn't run outside. *That's what the gym is for, right?*

Two hours later, Naomi was covered in sweat from her vigorous workout. She'd spent time running on the treadmill, then switched to doing squats and lifting some weights. Then she cooled off with some quick walking on the treadmill again.

She lifted her bottle of water to take a long drink and inhaled deeply to relax her heartbeat. *Phew! I need a shower — like now!*

She headed home and took a long, relaxing shower, pampering herself with her favorite scented soap. Then she sat in just a towel and did some writing on her latest story.

When she realized she was hungry, she stopped writing, and went into her bedroom to pull on a thong and a cotton shift. Then she threw a quick salad together, adding a hard-boiled egg and some blue cheese to it, along with some sunflower seeds. *Extra protein is good brain food, after all. And my brain is doing lots of work while I'm writing.*

She scrolled through her emails while she ate, then got

back to her writing. It was late afternoon when she finally stood up, stretching to work the kinks in her back out. She glanced at her watch to see how long she'd been writing and was surprised that it was already close to five. *Wow, I've been writing for most of the day! But I've got at least half of a new book done. Will, you're surely the best muse this gal could have. You inspire me!*

She looked out the window, noticing that the rainy drizzle that had been falling for most of the day had let up, and the sun was finally peeking through the clouds. *Hmm, I think I'll take a walk to the cafe on campus and get one of their yummy paninis. I can pair it with an iced coffee so I'll be alert enough to come back here and write some more. Maybe I can even finish the book today. Then I can spend a couple of days doing edits before I send it to my publisher.*

Satisfied that she had a plan, Naomi headed into her bedroom to change into shorts and a halter-top. She made a face at herself in the mirror as she pulled on her sandals. *No need for make-up. I'm not meeting anyone there. I just need to get out and be around people for a while. And the campus place is great for people-watching.* On her way out, she grabbed her phone and stuffed it into her tiny purse, then slung it over her shoulder. She grabbed her keys from the shelf by the door and headed out into the muggy afternoon to enjoy the sunshine.

Naomi was done with her sandwich and was savoring her iced coffee when she saw Will rapidly approaching her table. She smiled at him, but as he got closer, she was astounded by the haunted look on his face.

"Naomi! Ah'm glad te find ye here. We've got to go to the office." When she didn't get up, Will waved as if to encourage her to stand. "Now!"

"Why? You look like death warmed over, Will. What's going on?"

"Just get up. Ah'll explain while we walk."

Naomi rose and walked over to dump her trash into the container but kept her iced coffee. Will had followed her, and he loomed over her, a presence not to be denied.

He grabbed her elbow and began to lead her out of the crowd and onto the sidewalk. She was having trouble keeping up with his long legs.

"Will! Slow down! What's all this about?"

"There's nae time fer that, lass."

Naomi stopped. "There'd better be time for this. I'm not going anywhere with you until you explain yourself. What's the big hurry? And why do we need to get to the office?"

Will's face reflected his inner struggle. Naomi watched as emotions raged across his face, and his eyes changed from blue to black, then back again.

Finally, he sighed. "Yer right, lassie. Ye need to hear the truth. If we walk slower, will you come with me to the office?"

Naomi studied his face. His eyes at least appeared to be under his control again. "It's *them*, isn't it?"

"Aye. But will ye come?"

Naomi pursed her lips, then finally nodded. "Yes, I'll come. But you'd better start explaining yourself, mister."

They resumed walking at a more leisurely pace, though Naomi still had to work to keep up with Will's longer legs.

"Ye heard aboot the professor bein' hit by a car?"

"Yes, of course I did. Maggie called me. That's why I didn't have my appointment with him today. What does that have to do with anything?"

"Ah got called right after the accident. Ah went over to the 'ospital a wee while after that to sit in vigil for him. Ah dinnae know that many folks here. He's the same. His family is back in Chicago since his kids are still in school there. So Ah wanted there to be someone there to speak for him."

Naomi patted his arm. "That was sweet of you, Will. I'm sure when he's able to, he'll thank you for being there for him."

"Ah was there for hours. They finally got done patchin' him up around midnight. The nurses knew Ah was out there, so they sent a doctor out to talk to me. The doctor telt me Ah could go into his room but that he'd be unconscious and unable to answer me. He was badly injured. A few broken bones, lacerations, and a concussion. He was breathing fitfully. But as Ah watched him, the voices in mah heed started to whisper. Ah felt a headache buildin' and tried to ignore that. And the voices . . . Ah tried to ignore them, too. Then when Ah looked back at the professor, he grabbed ma arm with his one good hand and opened his een wide, while whisperin' to me. Ah didnae know what he was sayin', and Ah was sure this wasnae normal. Ah left to get a nurse, but by the time Ah got one to come back with me, he was lying still again. And the voices were in ma heed again. They got so loud Ah had to leave the room. Then Ah left the 'ospital because I couldnae hear what anyone else was saying. Ah could see their lips movin', but nae hear anythin."

"Why are they loud now?"

"Ah kept wondering that mahsel', all the way home. Then when Ah got to my apartment, the headache exploded. It was a blinding pain behind ma een. Like someone had a mallet and was in mah heed batterin' to get out. Ah tried a hot shower, trying to ease the tension, but it didnae help. Ah dinnae eat because Ah was too nauseated. Ah took some pain pills and went to bed hopin' rest would help."

"Did you feel better when you woke up?"

Will shook his head. "Nae, lassie. Ah kept havin' horrible dreams all night. Creatures Ah couldnae make oot were yelling at me, but Ah didnae understand what they were saying. They were so angry, and Ah was feart it was directed at me. Ah was feart to fall asleep again, then Ah would, and it would start all over again. It was after noon when Ah finally got oot of bed and took more pain pills fer the headache. Ah drank some water and lay doon again, trying to do deep breathing to make the pain stop. Suddenly Ah got a vision of you lying on the chair in the office. The voices were yelling at me. Ah watched mah hands working the controls, and suddenly it all made sense!"

"What made sense? I'm not following your logic, Will."

"It's nae logic, lassie. It's magic! It's the Unseelie in mah heed. They were showing me that *yer* the key! Yer the one Ah've been sent to find, and it's yer memories that are the key to what they need from me."

Naomi wrinkled her brow. "But how? I don't know anyone named Hamilton except for you."

"Not that ye know of, lassie. That's the point. The memories are locked in the last part of yer mind we havenae been in yet."

"You mean my early childhood memories? Maybe from before I was even in school? How can something that happened so long ago be important?"

"Ah hae ma suspicions, but Ah need proof. Fer that, we need to get to the office and use the equipment."

"But if your magic has been what made the equipment work, why do we need it? Why not just go to my apartment? Or yours?"

Will shook his head. "No. We need to be at the office, using the equipment and doing the procedures that have unlocked yer memories. That's how we'll access the ones we need."

"Then what? Will, I'm afraid of what we're going to find in there. Maybe we should just leave it be."

"Easy fer you to say, lassie. There are nae voices yelling in yer heed. But Ah cannae think of anything else until the pain and the voices stop. To do that, we need to hook you up to the machine and see what it is that's bothering you. Ah suspect it's what them in mah heed want us to see so they can see it also."

Naomi glanced at her watch. "It's after six already. Won't the building be closed this late?"

They were approaching the parking lot. Will waved his hand around at all of the cars still there.

"The building is nae closed up until after eight. After that, ye need a passkey and the permission of the security guard to get up there. But Ah have a passkey, and the guard's name is Frank. He'll let me up without any fuss. But since it's still early enough, we'll nae have to explain anythin' to him."

Naomi stopped. Will noticed she wasn't following him anymore and walked back to take both of her hands in his.

"Will, I'm scared." Naomi's words were whispered in a shaky tone.

"Ah know, lassie. But there's no hope for us to have any kind of relationship until this is finished. Ah have to do what Ah've been, um, *chosen* to do."

She must have shown she was still unconvinced, because Will leaned closer to her, speaking softly. "Ah've got a feeling that it's nae just *them* that's been waiting for *you*, and looking for *you*. Ah feel like mah life can finally really start now that Ah've found you."

Naomi looked into his eyes, getting lost in the light blue gaze he turned on her. "Really?"

He nodded. "Aye."

Naomi closed her eyes, taking deep breaths. She opened them to stare at the building, which suddenly appeared menacing. Finally, she shook her head and pulled her hands out of Wills.

"Then let's get in there and find out what this is all about."

Will led the way as they strode up to the front door and went into the building to find the answers they both needed.

CHAPTER FOURTEEN

Once they were in the office, Naomi watched as Will locked the outside door. He used another key to open the inner door that led to the room with the dream machines in it. She followed him in, still unsure. *Do I really want to do this?*

Suddenly she had a horrifying thought. What if the doctor was injured to stop her from finding out what was trapped in her earliest memories? *Shouldn't I just let it stay there?*

Will was getting the machinery ready for her to go under. He turned and smiled at her as he approached her with the wires to connect her.

"Ye look nervous, me lass. Don't be. Ah'm here with ye. Ah will nae let any harm come to you. Not when Ah have plans for us tae have a future together."

She could feel herself trembling. But his words surprised her, and she looked up into the blueness of his eyes and felt herself relax slightly. "Really?"

He nodded solemnly. "Aye."

She took a deep, calming breath as he attached the electrodes to her temples and forehead. He went back to the machinery and returned with the calming oil, handing it to her.

"Ye'll have to hold it under yer nose yersel', love. Ah've got to get the machine turned on. Then Ah'll touch it, and mah magic will flow into it so we can see what's so important in yer early memories."

She held the small jar of oil under her nose and breathed in deeply, then started to chant the mantra the doctor had taught her. This time she felt a small jolt as she fell into her dreams.

Is that Will's magic? I wonder why I never noticed it before. Maybe the doctor's presence masked it. She looked around. *Will? Are you here?*

"Aye, me love. Ah'm here with ye. Tell me where we're at."

"We're in my gramma's cottage. I used to stay here with her when I was three and Mom was working. My brothers were older, so they stayed at home. But I was sent here to be cared for by my gramma."

"It's a quaint wee cottage. Where's it located?"

"On the grounds of an antebellum mansion owned by the Reynolds family. My grandmother is their chef. She's lived here since she was a child herself. She raised her kids here."

"Did ye enjoy being here?"

"I was very young. I don't have many memories. At least not any I can call up easily. When Gramma talks about the time we spent together, I can sense images in my mind. I remember the smell of her house when she was teaching me how to bake cookies with her. I remember her reading me to sleep. I remember snuggling in her lap when I was afraid of the thunder and lightning of a storm."

"Ah, there ye are, tucked into bed. You were an adorable wee lassie."

Naomi jumped as she felt a hand tap on her shoulder. She turned quickly to see Cammy standing behind her, with Laird Duncan looming behind Will.

Duncan's eyes narrowed with suspicion. "Where's the other one? The old man with lust in his heart?" He moved closer behind Will. "And who's this one? Ah've ne'er seen him before." He spoke directly to Will. "Ye'd best remember she's protected in here by us. You dinnae belong in here. We live here. And we can hurt ye in here, if ye threaten our lady in any way."

Cammy turned to Will to appraise him. She smiled slowly, but only with her lips. She gave him a steely gaze. "What he's trying to say is that we decided to approach you to let you know we're here. No one hurts our Naomi — and certainly not here, in our domain."

Will nodded, holding his hands out to show he had no weapons.

"Ah've nae desire to hurt her — ever. On the contrary, Ah'm here with her to discover what's botherin' her. Ah suspect her memories are a threat to someone, who doesn't want her to remember something. Actually, Ah'm glad yer with us. Ah dinnae ken how to protect us both in here."

Suddenly they all became aware that little Naomi was waking up. She looked around, then got up out of bed. She walked over to the window and looked up at the bright moonlight streaming into her room. A slow smile spread across her face, and she walked over to open the door of her room. The moonlight was so bright she was easily able to navigate over to the front door of the house. She stood up on tiptoes to unlock it, then opened it and walked onto the porch.

She went down the stairs and looked around at the surreal appearance of everything around her. Trees glowed in the full moon's light. She could clearly see the path that led away from the cottage. She jumped when she turned and saw her own shadow on the ground. Then she giggled and began to dance with it.

"I wanna go play on the swings. Maybe Hannah will be there, and she'll sing so we can dance." She began to skip along the path that led away from the cottage. She picked a few flowers along the way and hummed a cheery song, mostly out of tune.

The others followed her quietly. Naomi was hyper-aware that she could feel a chill to the air, as if this was something she wasn't supposed to see. Cammy and Duncan were on guard, watching the surroundings as if they expected to be attacked at any moment. Will was either watching the younger version of her or studying her, as if he was trying to discern the meaning of this particular memory.

It didn't take long before they were at the playground. Naomi looked around in surprise, speaking her thoughts out loud. "Even as an adult with longer legs, it takes longer than this to walk here. How did we get here so quickly?"

"Ach, lassie, we're nae in real-time. We're in dream-time. Distance is nae as important as getting to whate'er it is we need to see."

She glanced at Will and nodded. They both turned to watch as little Naomi climbed on the monkey bars and jumped off of them. She got onto a swing but obviously hadn't learned yet how to pedal her feet. She wasn't able to get very high without anyone there to give her a push. She got off the swing and went over to the sandbox that had pails and shovels there, as well as small dolls that she made talk to each other as she moved them around.

Suddenly there was a crack of thunder off in the distance. The little girl looked up fearfully. She spoke in a tiny, shaky voice. "Hannah? Gramma? I don't wanna be alone anymore. Will someone play with me? Anyone?"

The only answer was another crack of thunder. Though it still sounded far away, it was obviously enough to terrify the small girl. She began to cry. She looked around for a place to hide. She got up and ran toward the bushes that surrounded the playground. "I hided in here when I played hide 'n' seek with Hannah. She'll find me."

Her observers watched as she crawled so deeply into the bushes that no part of her could be seen. But they could hear her fearful crying. She hiccupped whenever another crack of thunder was heard. Eventually, she grew quiet.

Cammy moved closer to the bushes, then returned to the others. "I hear gentle snoring. She's asleep."

Naomi looked around before asking, "Now what?"

Will took her hand. "We wait."

"For what? And for how long?"

Will shrugged. "Ah dinnae know fer what, nor fer how long. But it's dream-time, remember? Ah dinnae think we'll be waiting too long."

Naomi jumped when she was poked in the back by Cammy. "Hush, there's someone coming. Remember, they can't see or hear us. And we can only see what little-you did from your hiding place in the bushes. So, we may have trouble seeing everything — but maybe we can hear everything that's said."

Another crack of thunder was so loud it must have disturbed the sleeping child. A young blonde woman walked slowly along the path from the opposite direction that young Naomi had used. She looked around fearfully, as if she was unsure of something and hesitant to move out into the clearing.

Suddenly a large shape jumped out at her from the trees. "Boo!"

She shrieked, then a hand clamped over her face.

The others all watched as little Naomi opened her eyes and stretched. She peeked out of the bushes to see what had woken her.

"Careful, Hannah. We don't want to wake anyone else up, do we?" The man waited until she nodded, then he removed his hand from her mouth.

"Why not?" She appeared to be covering up her nerves with attitude. "What are you planning to do that can't be seen by anyone else?"

He grinned. "That's for me to know and you to find out."

"I still say we could have just gone on a date. It's not like my parents would disapprove. You live right next door, so they've known you your whole life."

He moved over to sit on the bench of the picnic table, patting next to him to indicate that she should join him.

She strolled casually closer, then sat as far from him as she could on the bench.

"Yes, but I'm not ready for anyone else to know that we're dating. Not yet."

"Why? Because you're always with other girls?"

He turned to her with unconcealed lust on his face. "There's no other girl for me, Hannah. Just you."

"That's BS!" She made a face at him. "You've got a reputation, you know. You date girls, make them love you, then you break their hearts. I don't even know why I agreed to meet you out here. I don't want to have anything to do with you and your tomcatting ways."

He moved closer to her on the bench. She was already on the edge, so there wasn't anywhere she could move without getting up. She tried to rise, but he grabbed her wrist and pulled her back down.

"Ow! Let go! You're hurting me."

"Oh, you know why you snuck out of bed in the middle of the night to meet with me, Hannah. You want a little excitement in your life. All the other boys treat you with kid gloves — like they're afraid of your family. But I'm not afraid of them. Or of anyone else."

He leaned closer and raised his hand to wrap it in her hair, pulling her face closer to his. "I'm the kind of man who takes what he wants. And right now, I want you, Hannah." He leaned closer to punish her lips with a violent kiss.

She struggled with him, trying to get away.

Suddenly he drew back. "You bitch! You bit me!"

"Keep your tongue in your own mouth, Daniel Worthington. I don't want any part of your nasty self inside of me."

He drew his hand back and slapped her across the face. "Oh, you don't? In case you haven't noticed, girlie, there's no one else out here except the two of us. And I'm bigger and stronger than you."

He moved closer to her and pulled her against his body, one hand wrapped in her hair to hold her in place, and the other roaming on her body, to begin to fondle her breast. "You know, I've heard locker-room talk that you're willing to suck a guy off, but you claim to be saving your cunt for your wedding night. Is that true, pretty Hannah? Are you still a virgin?"

She began to struggle harder, as if she realized now what he had planned. But no matter how hard she twisted and turned, he over-powered her. Soon he was ripping off her clothing, panting as he did.

"No one else has ever fought me this hard. What a hot piece of ass you're gonna be! You're a wildcat, babe!"

She continued to fight him, but it didn't do any good. It didn't take long for him to have ripped through her clothing. He took both of her wrists in his one hand and pulled his own pants open, then down. He pushed her over onto the ground and fell onto her.

Naomi was wide-eyed and whimpering with fear. The others watched the brutal scene unfold as her cries echoed those of the little girl watching in terror from the bushes.

The rape only lasted a few minutes. It took all of the fight out of Hannah. Soon she was crying softly, trying to pull her clothing back together.

Daniel slapped at her hands. "Oh no, you don't, you hot bitch. I'm not done with you yet."

"You've already gotten what you wanted from me. Leave me alone!"

"So you can run up to the house and tell everyone what happened?"

"No. I'm too humiliated to tell anyone. Just don't touch me again."

He sneered at her as he stroked himself with one hand, keeping her in place with the other. "Ah, but I'm going to. I want to try something that I read about. Did you know if you're being strangled, then you'll have a bigger orgasm? Let's try it!"

"No!"

He rolled back onto her. She tried to scream, but he held her down with one hand, wrapping the other one around her throat.

Both Naomis were whimpering more loudly, but there was a storm approaching – the wind whipping through the trees, and the approaching thunder drowned out the pitifully small sounds they were making.

Soon it was over. The man got up looking crazed. "That was the best I've ever had! Your cunt squeezed me so tight that I had to come way before I was ready. Was it good for you, too?"

When she didn't move, he nudged her with his foot. "Come on, Hannah. Stop pretending. Get up and face your lover. Tell me how good it felt. You know you wanted it. Was it as good as you thought? Or better? You know, if you ask me really nicely, I may let you suck me off, too."

He leaned over, anger making him yell louder. "Come on, bitch. Get up!" He pulled at her hands to make her stand, but she just fell over onto him, like a boneless rag doll. He shook her, his voice beginning to reflect fear. "Hannah! What's wrong with you? Open your eyes and yell at me. Cry. Do anything. But wake up."

He lowered her back onto the bench of the picnic table and felt her neck for a pulse. He lowered his head and put his cheek next to her nose. Then he stood up, looking around, his voice thin with panic.

"Oh shit! She's dead! What the fuck do I do now?" His head whipped around as he checked for witnesses. "No one saw anything. But I can't just leave her here. I've got to take her somewhere else . . .

somewhere far away from my house. I've got to make it look like she snuck out to meet some guy somewhere, and that's when she was killed. That's right. She's had lots of boyfriends. It could have been any one of them. But she never dated me. I'm safe." He pulled her up off the bench and threw her over his shoulder. Then he began to walk quickly along yet a third path leading away from the playground.

Adult Naomi looked around at Will, Cammy, and Duncan. Her eyes were wide open and filled with terror. She took in a staggered breath. "He killed her!"

Suddenly Naomi felt herself being pulled out of her dream so quickly that she was disoriented. She sat up quickly to look for Will, wondering why he'd broken the connection.

She gasped when she saw Daniel Worthington holding a gun to Will's temple. He turned to her with an evil smile that was only on his lips. His eyes blazed with the fury of insanity.

Chapter Fifteen

"You just had to keep at it, didn't you? You couldn't just let it go! I ran over that fucking doctor who was guiding you into your dreams. I thought that was the end of it. But just in case, I've been following you around. Imagine how I felt when I realized you two were heading into here to do what I didn't want you to do. Feel better now, bitch?"

"What difference does it make?" Naomi was watching his hand shake as he held the gun pointed at Will, who was standing perfectly still, staring at the floor. *I'm an author, damn it! I write scenes like this, and my heroes always get away alive. Think of something! Cammy? Duncan? Anyone?*

She tried to create a distraction, hoping that a way out of this situation would occur to her. "No one will believe us. And dreams can't be used as evidence against anyone."

He ogled her shamelessly, as if stripping her with his eyes. "You know, if you hadn't come to supper at the Reynolds place, I'd never have realized how close you were getting to discovering *our little secret.* I heard later that the young pickaninny that Hannah used to sit for was missing that night. But no one ever suspected that anything happened on the grounds. They found you at the playground. I wondered if you saw or heard anything. But as the years passed, I realized that you didn't. So I figured I was safe."

He raised his eyebrows to leer at her. "Ya know, you're one hot brown girl. I've never been across the color line. But for you, I'll make an exception."

Naomi forced herself to laugh. "Are you shitting me? You

think I'll let you touch me after what I just saw you do to poor Hannah? You're a twisted fuck. I'll enjoy seeing you put down."

Daniel grinned, shaking his head. "Um, who's the one with the gun, girlie? That would be me. And I've got it aimed at your boyfriend's head. But that's not where I'm gonna shoot him. I'll shoot him in the leg, so he won't be able to stop me from enjoying you. But he'll get to watch. Then after I get done with you, I'll shoot him a second time. It'll look like he forced his attention on you, and you shot him right before you gave up the ghost."

Naomi stared at Will, hoping to get him to meet her eye. But he wasn't looking at her. He appeared to be comatose, staring at the floor. So she turned her attention back to the murderer with the gun.

"You'll never get away with it, you know. They didn't have DNA typing back when you killed poor Hannah. But they do now. They'll discover that it wasn't Will who raped me. Then they'll come for you."

He shook his head, with a shrug, airily dismissing her. "So? They came for me when I was in college. There were a few *incidents* on campus. But it was *no big deal*. My parents paid a lot of money to lawyers and doctors, and I was found *not-guilty by reason of insanity*. They put me into an asylum. It was supposed to be for ten years. But you know the first thing I discovered? Nobody believes girls who are in there. Even when they say a man is groping them. Or saying nasty things to them. Hell, half the guards were fucking the ones who couldn't talk. But after I did a couple of them, I got bored. They weren't any challenge . . . no fight in them. So, I convinced the doctors that I was all better. More money changed hands, my parents sponsored a new wing to the place, and they let me out after only four years. And the best part about it? No one back here ever found out where I was for those four years."

He leered at her. "So don't worry about me, babe. I'll be fine. If they put me away again, I can deal with that."

Naomi was trying hard not to shake with terror because she sensed that he wanted to feed on her fear. Desperately she turned to look at Will again, hoping that he might be the key to her survival.

Daniel watched her trying to engage Will and laughed. "What? You think he's going to do something to save you? He's paralyzed with fear. He's worse than any girl I've ever scared the shit out of. He's not fighting. He's not struggling. He's just going to sit there and let me shoot him." He turned to Will and stroked his face with the gun. "Aren't you, pretty boy?"

Will looked up from the floor, and Naomi gasped. She'd seen his eyes do this before. There was no color — no blue, no white — only the blackness of pure evil in his eyes.

Even Daniel noticed it. "What the fuck is going on with your eyes, man? You'd better change them back to normal, or I'll shoot you in both of them instead of your leg. Because they're freaking me out, big time."

Will opened his mouth and his lips moved, but no sound came out. He took a deeper breath, and a puff of black smoke came out of his nostrils. He stared at Daniel, who grew visibly more agitated.

"Come on, asshole. Change your eyes the fuck back to normal, or I'll shoot your brains out right now."

Will began to speak in a halting, low voice that sounded like it had been left out to rust in the rain. "Daniel Worthington, sentence has been passed on you. You will pay for an eternity for your crimes."

Daniel's laughter had a maniacal edge to it. "Who's gonna make me pay, pussy boy? You? I'm the one with the gun, motherfucker." He leaned closer to Will and pulled the trigger.

Naomi squeezed her eyes tight, not wanting to see the damage a bullet to the brain could do to the man she was so fond of. When she didn't hear anything, she opened her eyes again to stare at the bizarre scene.

Will began to slowly advance toward Daniel, who was now holding the gun with both hands, pulling the trigger over and over, with nothing happening. He looked up when Will pointed at him with one arm extended.

"You are responsible for the rape, torture, and violent death of Hannah Reynolds. I am the seventh son of a seventh son of the Clan Hamilton. You are hereby cursed to spend the rest of eternity being tortured by the damned."

Daniel was cringing backward, trying to escape the blackness in Will's eyes, the stillness of his face, and his body that moved forward jerkily, as if it was being controlled by an unseen puppeteer. "You have no jurisdiction over me. Who are you to pass judgment on me?"

"I am the seventh son of a seventh son of the Clan Hamilton. You have been found guilty by your own admission. We saw in the dream what you did. You will spend the rest of eternity regretting your actions."

Daniel's voice was shrill. "Why should you care? She wasn't from your clan. She wasn't a Hamilton. She was a Reynolds."

"Her mother was born Elizabeth Hamilton. When you killed her child, you almost destroyed her. What you have done to two members of the Clan Hamilton is unforgivable. Prepare to meet your fate, Daniel Worthington."

Daniel threw his useless gun at Will and turned, trying to run. But he only got two steps away before he was unable to move anymore. "What have you done? Why can't I move my legs? This is like a fucking bad dream, where the bad guys are coming for you and you can't run away. But this isn't a dream.

It's real. You need to go away and leave me alone!"

Will advanced so close that his face was right in front of Daniel's. Daniel was trying to turn his face away, but Will put his hands on either side of his head to hold him still. He intoned strange words in his raspy, deep voice that was joined by other voices, as if multiple beings were using his vocal cords, all at the same time. Daniel looked too petrified to move.

The effect was so horrifying that Naomi couldn't move either. All she could do was watch. She had to force herself to remember to breathe.

Will's hands now pulled Daniel's face closer so that their foreheads touched. Will opened his mouth, and Naomi was certain that she saw black smoke coming out of him. Daniel's mouth gaped open in horror, and the black smoke entered through his mouth and his nostrils. He began to shake violently, as if he was trying to fight off what was happening to him.

He whimpered. "No! I didn't do it! You can't touch me! I'm a Worthington! My family has money. No one can touch me! Let me go! No! Ow! That hurts! Ouch! Leave me alone!"

His voice became weaker as more of the blackness entered into him.

Suddenly Will began to sway.

Naomi forced her body to respond, moving over to put a chair behind him. He fell backward into the chair, his head lolled back, and he fainted.

She turned to look at Daniel, who was staring wide-eyed but seeing nothing.

He moved backward jerkily, as if not in control of his body anymore. He ended up sitting on one of the benches. His mouth was still open and moving, but no words came from him. He whimpered quietly, his face frozen in a rictus of horror. His eyes were unfocused, as if he was seeing things that weren't physically there. And what he *was* seeing was obviously terrifying. Naomi watched as a wet spot formed on the front of his pants to spread down his legs, and a long spittle of drool began to leak from his open mouth as he panted in short, shallow breaths.

Naomi was scared to death, so she turned away from the awful fate that the murderer had brought on himself. She saw Will beginning to stir.

She moved over to kneel in front of him, clasping his hands in hers. "Will? Will, are you all right? Talk to me, honey. Say something."

A slow grin spread across his face, deepening his dimples. "Lassie, did ye just call me *honey*?" He opened his eyes.

Naomi was relieved to see the brilliant color that made her want to drown in their clear, light blueness. "So what if I did, mister?"

He smiled. "Hopefully, *they* have *all* gone—and Ah can woo ye like Ah've been dreaming aboot since Ah met ye."

Naomi rolled her eyes. "Woo me? What, are we in one of my Laird Duncan novels? Because that sounds kind of old-fashioned—"

She didn't get to finish what she was saying because Will leaned forward to kiss her. She suddenly realized she didn't care *how* he said it, as long as it finally happened.

Chapter Sixteen

Naomi used the office phone to call the police to report an intruder had broken into the doctor's office with a gun, but he'd been neutralized.

While she and Will waited, they agreed on what they would say. So when the police appeared, led in by the security guard George, they both told the same story — repeatedly.

The lead detective frowned at them both, as they sat in the patient's chairs in front of the doctor's desk. "So you say that you were *in her dream*, and you have no idea how this man got into the office or what he wanted?"

Will and Naomi both nodded.

Will leaned forward. "Ah'm the professor's lab assistant. Ah've been helping him go into her dreams, trying to figure out what was causing her to have anxiety attacks in public. She only had the one session to go, but the doctor was in a hit-and-run yesterday."

Naomi nodded. "That's right. So when he walked into the cafe on campus, where I was having dinner, we talked about trying to do it without him, just to finish things off."

The detective glared at both of them. "In your dreams, right? That's where you both were. And what did you find? Did you get your answers?"

Naomi shook her head. "No. I just watched myself as a little girl, sneaking out at night and playing on a playground until I got tired. Then I fell asleep under some bushes. I was there until my grandmother came to find me."

"And when Ah disconnected us both from the machinery,

this man was here in the office. Ah'd locked the outer door when we got here, so Ah dinnae know how he got in."

"The evidence guys said it had been jimmied open . . . obviously by a clumsy amateur. But did he give you any reason for being here? And for having a gun?"

Both Will and Naomi shook their heads.

Will spoke. "He didnae say anythin'. He threw the gun at me, then he fell onto that bench and started whimpering. He's been like this" — he waved his hand toward the comatose man — "ever since then."

"Do either of you have any idea who he is? Have you ever seen him before?"

Naomi spoke slowly, as if she wasn't sure. "He looks different now, but I think I met him last weekend."

The detective gave her his undivided attention. "Continue."

"I was spending the weekend with my mom, visiting *her* mother. She lives on the grounds of the Reynolds place, a couple of hour's drive from here. She's the chef for the Reynolds family. They invited Mom and me to supper on Sunday night. And he was there. His name is Daniel . . . Daniel Worthington. His family owns the place next to the Reynolds' land. He's friends with their son, Harold."

She wrinkled her brow. "At least, I think it's him. It's hard to tell because he looks so . . . so tortured. Do you have any idea what's wrong with him?"

"We were hoping you two could shed some light on that. As it is, we're having him taken to be evaluated. I guess we'll contact the Worthington family to see if they can tell us anything."

The detective was called over to talk on the phone, leaving Will and Naomi alone for a minute.

Will leaned over and grabbed Naomi's hand to kiss the back of it. He smiled at her, and she felt the warmth of his feelings wash over her. She smiled back. They both looked up when the detective returned.

Will spoke up. "So are we free to leave?"

The detective snorted as he shook his head. "Ah, nope. You both need to come down to the station to give your statements."

"But we've already told you all we know." Naomi was trying to look persuasive.

"Yeah, but not your official statements that will need your signatures."

"How long is all of that going to take?" Naomi smiled at Will for asking what she had been thinking.

The detective shrugged. "Maybe only a couple of hours. Maybe longer." Noticing their raised eyebrows, he smirked. "It depends."

"On what?" Naomi asked.

"On how busy the station is, on who's available to take your statements. And on how cooperative you two are as witnesses."

Looking up, he nodded at the uniformed policewoman who had approached them. He turned back to them. "You'll be driven in separate cars to the station."

"Um, why?" Will asked.

Naomi patted his arm. "To be sure we're not concocting a story to tell them when we get there, Will."

The detective gave her a sharp look. "How do you know that?"

The policewoman waved at her. "Don't you recognize her? She's Delu Morris, the author. She writes a series about a female secret agent. She's good about keeping things accurate when she writes about standard police practices. So she knows what she's talking about." She turned to Naomi and held out her hand. "I'm so pleased to meet you, Ms. Morris."

Naomi shook her hand, looking at her badge. "And you're

Officer Kane? Lead the way, officer."

As they were leaving, Naomi saw a male uniformed police-man come to collect Will, to drive him to the station also.

Their statements ended up taking up most of the night. *After all*, Naomi reasoned, *they've got to be here all night. There's no reason for them to care how long it takes. It's not way past their bedtimes.*

She heard Cammy blow a long raspberry in her head and smiled. Feeling her phone chirp, she pulled it out of her pocket and read the text.

Might be let go soon. Too tired. Need to get some sleep. I've fallen asleep twice already. Can we do dinner tomorrow night?

She replied. *Yes! When?*

I'll pick you up at six.

You know where I live?

I've walked by it many times, daring myself to knock on your door. So, yes.

She sent him back a smiling emoji with hearts in its eyes. *See you then.* As an afterthought, she sent another message. *What should I wear?*

A dress? I'll be wearing ma kiltie.

The tingle she felt made her toes curl and her nipples tighten. This time her response was a throbbing heart emoji.

The female police officer came back to tell her she was ready to give her a ride home.

Naomi was too tired to even brush her teeth. She quickly stripped, pulled on her nightgown, and was asleep before her head even hit the pillow. And when she dreamed, it involved lots of running across the Highland moors toward a dark-haired man wearing a kilt, playing the bagpipes.

CHAPTER SEVENTEEN

Naomi slept in the next morning, and when she finally woke up, it was after nine. She toasted some bread and spread half an avocado on it, then topped it with a poached egg. While she ate, she pondered over yesterday's events.

She had to stop herself from calling her mother and her grandmother. *After all, I can't tell them what really happened. Not that they'd believe me anyway. And on the off-chance they did, that would put Gramma, especially, in such an awkward position. She sees Mrs. Reynolds every day. It would be agony for her to know what really happened to Hannah and to be unable to tell her. The comfort she might get from knowing that the murderer is being punished eternally by the Unseelie would be made worse by knowing what had actually happened to her beloved daughter.*

No, it's best that I keep this to myself. But it will sure be hard! I'm just glad that I can talk about it with Will — at least there's one person who will understand my situation.

After breakfast, she went to the gym and spent a couple of hours tiring her body out, trying to work off the tension of seeing the supernatural at work. No matter how she pushed herself, the image of Will's black eyes, the black smoke that moved from him into Daniel, and the resultant damage done to the murderer, no matter how well-deserved it was, kept her nerves tingling with anxiety.

When she got home, she took a long, hot soak in a bubble bath. Afterward, she painted her toenails and moisturized her hair. Then she tried to do some writing. When her stomach began to rumble, she called out for a delivery of some falafel and hummus from her favorite middle eastern place. She scrolled through the news while she ate, then she sat down to write again. She was frustrated by the lack of inspiration from her muse as to how to continue her current Laird Duncan story.

She got up and stretched, then was overcome by a huge yawn. Maybe she needed a nap. She needed to catch up on her beauty sleep. She wanted to be at her best when she finally went out on her first date with her sexy Scotsman. She smiled.

She lay down on her bed and was asleep almost instantly.

She dreamed of being captured and held by those who wanted to ransom her – after they raped her. She was crying, sure that no one could possibly come to her rescue. Suddenly she heard fighting going on in the next room. Finally, when things quieted down, she looked up in alarm when the door was opened. Her cousin, Laird Duncan, walked in, followed by a tall, dark-haired man with piercing blue eyes.

"How did you find me?" she whimpered.

Laird Duncan cut open the ropes that bound her wrists and ankles. He pulled her up, pointing to the man behind him. "Let me introduce Will Hamilton. He found you using the Gaelic magic of the islands, lassie. He's the seventh son of a seventh son."

Her eyes met the steady, lustful gaze of the tall man, and she was lost, drowning in the depth of the twin blue flames of his eyes.

She stumbled toward him, her legs unsteady after having been restrained for so long. He caught her in his strong arms. Using one hand, he tilted her head up and crushed her lips with a passionate kiss.

Naomi woke with a gasp.

That's it! She needed some magic in her latest Laird Duncan story. And maybe a tall, dark-haired magic man in a kilt.

She went into the next room and turned her laptop on again. The words flowed from her fingers as the story came to life.

When Naomi looked at the time, three hours had gone by. She got up, stretching again, and realized that if she was going to be picked up at six, she needed to decide what she was going to wear and begin getting ready.

She took a long time to decide what to wear. After trying on most of what she owned, she chose her favorite slinky dress. It was made of gold satin that hugged her curves. It had tiny spaghetti straps that held up her breasts and sewn-in pads that were meant to hide her nipples. But that never really worked. The gown also had a low back, with ties that held it in place across her middle back. There was a slit up one side that went up to her mid-thigh. And she paired it with gold pumps with low heels. She chose a large pair of gold hoop earrings to finish the look.

When the doorbell rang, she took one last glance at herself in her full-length bedroom mirror. *Lookin' good, girlie.* She smiled, remembering her mother's words whenever she'd dressed for a date while in high school.

Then she strode quickly over to open the door. As she gazed at the man, she realized she wasn't breathing, so she tried to cover her gasp as her lungs forced her to supply them with oxygen.

Will was wearing his clan's kilt but in a more formal style than she'd seen before. His kilt was red with three dark blue stripes and a single white stripe as the markings for the tartan. He was wearing a white shirt with flowing sleeves that ended in wide cuffs with gold cufflinks. His tie matched his kilt, and he was wearing a double-breasted vest in the same blue that was on his kilt, with gold buttons. It enhanced the color of his eyes. He wore a black leather sporran in the front of his kilt and blue socks with flashes on them that had strips that matched his kilt. His black shoes completed his outfit.

Naomi forced herself to look back up and into Will's face. His eyes were intense as they swept over her. Suddenly realizing that one of them had to say something, Naomi cleared her throat. "Um, you look great!"

His eyes still burned as his lips curled upward slightly. "And you take mah breath away, lassie."

Naomi smiled shyly. "So you like my dress?"

He nodded slowly. "Ach, aye. But even more, Ah appreciate the beauty of the woman in the dress."

Her eyes widened, her breath sped up, and she could feel her pulse beginning to race. "Um, do we have reservations?"

He glanced at his watch, then his face reflected disappointment. "Aye, that we do. And Ah've heard that ye need to be on time at The Black Hen. So as much as Ah'd like to just stand right here, in awe of yer loveliness, Ah'm afraid we have to get going."

Naomi reached for her purse and her keys, both of which were on a small side table by her door. She stuffed her phone into the small gold bag and smiled. "Then let's not be late."

She walked through the door and pulled it closed, then locked it. She could feel heat emanating from behind her and knew that it was Will. She took a deep breath and turned around. His eyes burned into hers as he lifted one arm. His hand tilted her chin up before he leaned over to cover her lips with his.

As he deepened the kiss, she leaned closer to him, meeting his passion with equal fervor. She opened her lips but whimpered when he pulled back to rest his forehead on hers.

"Ach, Naomi, what ye do to me. That will have to hold us until we return here later."

She swallowed hard, nodding. "Okay. As long as I know there will be a later."

He lifted one eyebrow as one of his dimples deepened.

"Och, aye. That's fer certain."

He held out his crooked arm, and she wrapped her hand around it to walk with him to the elevator.

Two hours later, they were finishing their meal. In the car on the ride there, they'd discussed the fact that they shouldn't talk about their recent adventure while in a public place where they could be overheard. So their dinner conversation was about general things they were both interested in, like the history of Will's clan in Scotland.

As they sipped their after-dinner coffee, waiting for the dessert menu, Will leaned over to cover Naomi's hand with his. "Ah do have an important question to ask ye, me love."

Naomi looked up quickly into his eyes. "Oh? What might that be?"

Will took a deep breath. "Will ye come to Scotland with me to meet mah family?"

Naomi nodded. "I'd love to. But first, you have to meet mine. After all, they're a lot closer than yours."

Will's dimples deepened. "Ah'd be honored to meet them. But ye see, Ah'm thinking o' transferrin' to the University of Edinburgh. Ah'd like to change mah major back to technology and finish mah graduate degree in that."

"So, no more psychology? Won't Doctor Banning be upset?"

Will smirked. "Ah dinnae expect so. Especially once he realizes that his machinery willnae work anymore, even with me at the controls."

"Do you think he might accuse you of having broken it?"

"Ah've already explained things to him. About how we were pulled suddenly out of yer dream, only to find that we were nae alone in the office anymore. Who knows what that person did to the machinery while we were unaware?"

Naomi nodded. "Yes, who knows? And I hope his

disappointment over not being able to help me discover the source of my anxiety will be at least somewhat eased by the fact that I'll be willing to spread the word about how his procedure helped me to discover ways to deal with it. A high-profile ex-patient like myself is good to have as a reference. But if he were to make trouble for you? Well, then, I wouldn't be so willing to provide a glowing review of his analytical skills."

Will grinned. "Ah, yer a cunning wench. Any man who goes up against ye had best have his wits about him."

"I'd like to have *you* up against me." Naomi was shocked by the words that had come out of her mouth. *Where did that come from?*

The answer came in a bark of laughter from Cammy. *"You're welcome, honey. Get to it! You don't need dessert. What you do need is time to be alone with your sexy Scotsman!"*

Will had leaned over closer to her, his hand on her shoulder, stroking her skin with his fingertips as they made their way up her neck to her ear. His face grew closer, and Naomi moved so that their lips were almost touching.

She licked her lips, excited by the intake of breath she heard from him. "Maybe we don't need the dessert menu after all?"

His lips pressed against hers gently. His tongue licked at the seam of her lips, and she opened them with a sigh. The kiss deepened as they both leaned closer. Slowly he drew back, smiling at the look on her face.

"Aye. Mah appetite isnae fer anythin' on the menu anymore."

Naomi's voice was a breathy whisper. "Is it *later*?"

He nodded solemnly. "Aye."

Their waiter appeared with the menu, which Will waved away. "We willnae be needin' that. Please bring us our check."

The drive back to Naomi's apartment was an anomaly. It

went by in a blur because Naomi wasn't paying attention to her surroundings. She was imagining what it would be like to finally be able to touch the man she'd been lusting after for so long. But at the same time, the drive seemed to take forever.

When they finally got to her building, she directed him to the parking garage, since he'd parked on the street to pick her up.

"That way, your car won't be ticketed if it's here longer." *Like overnight!*

Will expertly drove up the levels to find a parking spot. Once he did, he turned off the car and walked around to her door, which she'd already opened. He reached inside to take her hand and pulled her up to stand in front of him.

"Ah've been waiting so long for this," he said before crushing her lips with his.

His hands traveled around to stroke the skin of her back. She pressed against him, and her hands went up his chest to his shoulders, then around the back of his neck to play with his hair while pulling his head closer to her.

They were oblivious to anything else until a car door slammed very nearby, and a voice could be heard saying, "Isn't she that author?"

Naomi pulled back from the kiss to whisper, "Pictures. Phones have cameras. We don't want to be all over the internet."

He nodded, pulling her back to shut his car door. Holding hands, they made their way to the elevator to take them to her floor. Luckily there were already other people in the elevator when they got into it, so the ones who had recognized her had to wait for the next car.

CHAPTER EIGHTEEN

Naomi's nerves were thrumming with anticipation. She could feel her nipples beading against the dress, the silky feel of the fabric only enhancing their sensitivity. She could feel the moisture leaking between her legs. The ride to her floor seemed to take forever. Finally, they got off and walked quickly to her door.

She fumbled with the lock but finally got the door open. She fell through it with Will right behind her. She turned to shut and lock the door.

Will moved her hair aside and kissed her neck, whispering in her ear, "At last, Ah've got you to mysel'. Ah've been waiting for this since the first time Ah saw you." His tongue explored the taste of her skin before he nipped at her earlobe.

Naomi was trembling, shivering through arousal so intense she wasn't sure she'd be able to speak. She drew in a long breath. "I've wanted you since I saw you in your kilt that first time."

Will backed off, and she turned to feel herself pressed against the door, Will's arousal hard against her, as his lips crushed hers. He drew back to lick at her lips, and she opened for him with a sigh. His tongue thrust into her mouth, and she reveled in the feeling of being consumed by him, as well as by her own passion. Their tongues dueled, caressing each other, exploring the taste of each other.

Will ran his hands down from her waist to her hips, then pulled her even more tightly against his erection, causing her to rub herself against him and moan.

Naomi's hands were on his shoulders before moving up his neck to play with the hair on his nape. She tugged on it, and he groaned.

Will drew his face back to rest his forehead against hers as he stared into her eyes.

She felt a sudden terror when his eyes appeared to be black again. Then she looked more closely to see the corona of light blue that surrounded his hormonally-enlarged pupils.

He looked drugged as he asked in a rasp, "Bedroom?"

She smiled seductively. "Come with me."

"You first." He smiled. "But aye, Ah was plannin' on that, too."

She giggled, then took his hand and led him down the hall to her bedroom.

Once they were near the bed, he took over doing the leading, walking backward until his legs were stopped by the mattress. His lips found hers again before he trailed them along her face to her ear, then down her neck. He licked at her skin, using his teeth to pull the spaghetti strap off her shoulder. Then his tongue trailed a path up to her neck again and over to the other shoulder. His teeth pulled that side off also. The top of the dress fell, revealing her breasts.

Will sat down hard on the bed and pulled her closer to him, fastening his mouth to one nipple while he toyed with the other one. He alternately licked, sucked, and bit the nipple, while twisting and pulling on the other one.

Naomi was writhing in his arms.

He looked up at her and an evil grin swept across his face as his mouth and hand changed places, and he proceeded to torture her other nipple, while using his hand on the other one. His other hand unzipped the back of her dress, and it fell to her feet.

"Will, please . . ." Naomi wasn't able to make enough words come out of her mouth to explain what she needed.

Will inhaled deeply before he licked at the sweat trickling down between her breasts. His hands traveled down her body, both of them ending up on her hips, now wearing only a lace thong. Gently, he eased it down her legs, and she kicked off her heels when she lifted each leg to get out of the thong. He took a deep breath as he gazed at her naked body, before whispering, "Yer beautiful." One hand moved down to toy with her curls, before he dipped a finger between her lower lips and swirled her moisture around. "Is this what ye want, lassie?" He tapped at her clit, making her gasp. "Or is this?" He slid his longest finger into her, exploring her.

Naomi began moving her hips, panting in search of relief from her own arousal.

Will inserted a second finger, moving his hand to use his fingers to search for the elusive spot on her inner walls. He moved both of them in and out, occasionally swirling them around.

Naomi stopped moving for just a split second before she gasped as her body trembled through the release of her orgasm. She rode his still-moving hand, twitching through the after-shocks of her sudden pleasure. Then she stilled, using her hands to pull on the hair at the back of his head, forcing his face up to meet her kiss.

"I need to see you naked," she said on a moan.

He nodded at her, licking his fingers. "Yer taste is addictive, woman." He turned to pat the bed beside him. "Sit doon. Ah've way too much clothin' on, and some of it is hard to get off. Allow me to strip for yer pleasure."

He stood close enough for her to touch as he removed his jacket first. She reached up to unravel his tie. Then she undid the buttons on his vest, and he shrugged out of it.

She tore at the buttons on his shirt. Then she pulled the ends of his shirt out from being tucked into his kilt, and leaned back on her elbows to leer at him. "Yes," she hissed.

"Now you're truly the Scotsman of my dreams."

His eyes twinkled, and his dimples deepened. He threw the shirt aside.

Her gaze was fixed on the obvious sign of his arousal that tented the front of his kilt, as he undid the belt to remove the sporran.

He paused for a moment. "Do Ah need a condom?"

She grinned. "Why? Is that what you carry in there?"

He nodded. "Tonight, aye."

She shook her head. "I have an IUD. I checked out clean at my last doctor visit, and I haven't been with anyone in a very long time. But then, you've been in my dreams, so you know that."

"And Ah've nae been with a lassie since Ah realized Ah was carrying the wee folk in ma heed."

Once he dropped the sporran to the floor, the tent in his kilt was clearly visible. In a breathy voice, she murmured, "I've always wondered what a Scotsman has under his kilt."

"Ach, lassie. 'Tis a wee set o' bagpipes."

She reached her hands out, one pulling him closer so she could lift his kilt, the other grasping what was revealed. "Not so wee."

He smirked. "Ach, it's a caber now. That's the way it's been ever since Ah met ye."

She leaned closer, lowering her head to lick at the drop leaking out of the tip. She looked up at Will's gasp, then used her tongue to spend a few long moments exploring him.

He groaned as he dug his fingers into her scalp. "Ah cannae hold mahsel' back. Ah have to have ye now!" he groaned, as he pushed her backward onto the bed.

She inched her way up so that her feet no longer touched the floor, and he got onto the bed to crawl on his hands and knees, a lion seeking its prey. He knelt between her thighs, using his knees to spread them wide. He pulled a pillow over to put it under her hips, then began to rub himself in her wetness. His eyes were almost black — wild with passion. "Ach, Naomi, Ah willnae last long this first time. Ah've wanted you for far too long. But that will only be the beginning of our night."

Once again, Naomi was shocked to hear what came out of her mouth. "Just take me, Will, and don't be gentle. I want to be ravished by my sexy Scotsman." This time she heard multiple giggles in her mind, as if Cammy was joined by the various maidens who'd enjoyed Laird Duncan. *Are they all going to watch?*

Then thinking became impossible as Will took her at her word. He slammed himself into her, and Naomi saw stars as she stopped breathing. "Yes! More!"

He grunted his acknowledgment as he began to piston in and out of her while twisting both of her nipples. Then one hand moved downward, and his longest finger sought the bud of her pleasure. Naomi felt herself climbing up an enormous hill, then he pinched her clit, and she screamed as she shattered.

Will continued his assault. His hands moved to grip her hips, holding her closer to him, until he pulled her flush against himself and roared out his pleasure. He hung suspended for a heartbeat, before collapsing forward onto her.

Naomi felt her breath whoosh out of her, but she was able to continue with the shallow panting she was doing, as her heartbeat slowed back down to normal. Her hands idly stroked his back, from his wide shoulders, down to his narrow waist. She alternated using her fingertips, then her nails.

Will's butt muscles tightened. His voice held humor as he spoke almost into her ear. "Ye willnae give me any time to rest *in-between*, will ye, lassie?" He rolled off to the side, pulling her with him so she was lying on top of him. He used one knee to spread her thighs so her mound pressed directly onto him, where she could feel a still sizable erection, despite his recent release.

She lifted her head to gaze into his face. "Apparently, you don't need any time, mister."

He reached up to wrap one hand in her hair, to pull her down for a long, exploratory kiss. Then he rolled her over onto her back, and he rested his head on one of his hands, while using the other to glide along every inch of her skin that he could reach, smiling as she twitched. "Not with you, Naomi. We've only begun to explore the ideas Ah've had in mah heed since meetin' you."

She smiled at him. "Eventually, I'll get thirsty from so much moaning and panting and screaming. Should I just get up now and bring in a bottle of champagne? And maybe some cheese and crackers for when we need to replenish our energy?"

"That's a good idea. I'll come with you to help you carry ai' that back. And that way, we can both use the loo before round two."

She giggled. "You're a poet, and you don't know it."

"Remind me someday to show you some of the poetry Ah've written during the long nights when Ah couldnae sleep fer wantin' you."

She raised one eyebrow. "Another writer in the family?"

He shook his head. "Ah dinnae think so, lassie. Just a poor, lonely, love-struck Scotsman who was afraid he'd never get a chance with the bonnie lass who'd caught his fancy."

She grasped his cock, giving it a long stroke. "Your fancy? Is that what you call it?"

He growled at her, and she mock-shrieked as she scooted over to the other side of the bed and darted for the door.

Will moved more quickly than she'd have thought possible and pulled her against him.

She inhaled deeply against his chest, giggling as his chest hair tickled her nose. Will's hands were busy exploring her curves.

She tilted her head up to look into his eyes, relieved to see that the light blue color had reasserted itself. "You had me worried for a minute. Your eyes were almost all black again for a while. But now they're back to normal."

He answered with a grin. "Ma pupils must expand, along with another part of me, whenever Ah'm near you. Ah'm nae sure, but Ah'm hoping the wee folk are done with me."

"*They* may be, but I'm not. Let's go get that snack we'll both need. Then we can get back to exploring each other in a more leisurely manner."

She turned, and he gently slapped her ass. "Let's get to it, lassie. Ah've been patient far too long. Ah intend to pleasure you until you beg me to stop . . . until there's no memory of any other man in yer heed."

Her smile spread across her face as she led him down the hall. She glanced back over her shoulder. "Getting you *and* an extended visit to Scotland? I'm a lucky woman. And you've inspired me to start writing again."

"Ah have? Then we'd best get back to inspiring you."

And they did.

EPILOGUE

"Tell me again why Ah have to be in mah full-dress kiltie, wife."

Naomi smiled as she adjusted her husband's tie. "Because we're being honored by a very old, very proud southern family. They're throwing us a reception to celebrate our marriage."

"But they're the ones who employ your gran as their cook."

"Chef," she corrected him automatically. "But for tonight, she'll be a guest also. They're having this event catered." She admired how he looked as he pulled on his jacket to complete his look. "Seeing you dressed like this reminds me of the first time I saw you in a kilt . . . the first time we met. And then the first time I saw you in your full-dress regalia. That time I got to watch you remove it, piece by piece."

He glared at her. "Ach, woman, we'll no be going anawhere if you keep talking like that. Ah'll have to have mah way with you."

"Again?" Her eyes sparkled with amusement. "Then we'd just have to shower again and get dressed. No, it's better if we just go and make nice with the Reynolds family and their guests. We can come back here later, and *then* I'll let you have your way with me as many times as you can manage."

He growled. "That sounds like a challenge . . . to see *how many* times."

She grinned. "Aye, laddie."

She walked over to the door of their honeymoon suite, and he loomed behind her as she unlocked the door, pressing himself into the curve of her butt. "How long do we have to stay?"

"Will! They've gone to a lot of trouble to honor us tonight. The least we can do is stay for a couple of hours after dinner."

"So for two hours after we're done eating?"

"Honestly, you'd think we were still on our honeymoon, the way you're acting!"

"Ach aye, Ah feel like we are. Ah cannae get enough of you to ever feel satisfied, wife."

"Good. I hope you always feel like that. But we didn't invite the Reynolds to our wedding, so they didn't get the chance to share in our happiness last year. So when I proposed we come back to the states to celebrate Mom's birthday, Gramma mentioned it to the family, and they promptly decided they wanted to throw a celebration for us. And I figure it's the least they can do to thank you for what you did for them—even though, of course, they have no idea what that was."

When they got to the lobby of the hotel, a driver was there waiting for them. He touched his hat in respect, then nodded toward the limousine parked right outside the door.

After he opened the door and they both slid onto the buttery soft seats, he shut the door and got into the driver's seat. He eased out of the driveway to begin the drive from their hotel to the Reynolds estate.

Will looked around with wide eyes. "There's a wee fridge in here? Ah wonder what's in it?"

Naomi waved at the ice bucket that had an opened bottle of champagne in it, with two glasses next to it on the tray next to the fridge. "Probably some cheese for us to nibble on as we sip our champagne." She poured some into each glass and handed one to Will.

They clinked their glasses together and took a sip.

"This tastes expensive," Will remarked.

"I'm sure it is. They're pulling out all of the stops tonight."

"Why? Just because you're the daughter of their cook? Ah mean, chef?"

She smirked. "That, and the fact that I'm a famous author. And the story of how we were attacked by a man who somehow destroyed Doctor Alan's machinery made the papers even here."

"Am Ah right in thinking that the next-door neighbors willnae be invited to this event? After all, that *man* was their kin."

Naomi nodded. "Yes. Gramma says there's no contact between the families right now. She's sad that such long-time friends are estranged. But she's hopeful that with the passage of time, that will heal over." She poured more wine into both of their glasses. "But to answer your original question, this will be in the society pages for weeks. There will be pictures taken. That's why you had to be in your full-dress kilt kit. And why I have to wear a gown with real heels—even though I'll be worried all night that I'll fall off of them."

Will ran his hand along her thigh, making her shiver. "Ah'll be there to catch you, ma love. Always."

"Good. Now I haven't eaten since breakfast, so let's see what's in the mini-fridge."

He leaned forward to open the door, then turned to her with a smile. "Ach aye, civilization has come to the colonies." Will pulled out a labeled cheese board. "There's a wee dod of English blue and some Gloucestershire. There's also an aged Irish cheddar—well, we can forgive them for *that* one. And a dollop of currant jam to go with the tea biscuits."

"So, you approve?"

He was already savoring some of the flavors when he nodded. "Ach aye. But Ah still expect to only spend a couple of hours after dinner, as you promised. Then we have important business to attend to." He arched his brows up and down, leering at her before he winked.

"If they've taken as much care with the dinner food as they have with our appetizers, I think we're going to enjoy being the guests of honor for the night."

"Never-the-less, Ah'll no be wasting ma whole night making small talk with society folks Ah dinnae know. Not when we can get another long soak in that king-sized whirlpool tub in our honeymoon suite."

"Yes, it was lovely of Mom and Dad to put us up there, wasn't it? Such a thoughtful gesture."

He smiled and nodded, helping himself to some of the jam and biscuits. "Aye, i' twas at that. And you thanked them for us, nae doot?"

Naomi rolled her eyes. "Yeah. Then I had to listen to *my own mother and grandmother* make lewd comments about how much, *back in the day*, they would have enjoyed such a huge bed with a mirror on the ceiling — and the huge Jacuzzi. Seems they both looked at the pictures of the amenities on the hotel's website. Honestly, I know theoretically that they both enjoyed sex when they were younger, but why on earth they have to tell me about it is beyond me!"

Will snorted with amusement, leaning forward to feed her one of the biscuits with jam.

As she crunched it, he leaned even closer and covered her lips with his. "Ah hope you willnae be sharing any details of our intimate moments with them. Ah'd ne'er be able to look your faither in the een again!"

Naomi leaned back in her seat and smiled innocently.

Will rolled his eyes at her assumed impropriety.

They continued to enjoy the snacks and the wine, as well as the banter, making the time pass enjoyably.

Before the limo stopped, Naomi opened the window to point at the small cottage they passed.

"That's yer gran's cottage, right?"

She nodded. "Yes, but how did you know?"

"Ah saw it in yer dreams, remember? It looks the same as it did back when you were a wee bairn. "

"I'm not sure if she's still there right now. Mom and Dad may be there with her since they're staying with her tonight. But Mrs. Reynolds said she wanted us to get to the mansion before everyone else so we would be more relaxed when the place gets crowded."

Will sighed loudly. "Ach, the things a man must do for love."

Naomi patted his knee. "You poor, long-suffering man." Her hand began to travel up his thigh, under his kilt.

He slapped her hand away. "There'll be nane of that, lassie, unless you want me pole-vaulting into the mansion with mah caber at full attention."

The limo stopped, and when the door was opened, the driver studiously looked the other way since his passengers were smooching.

Naomi drew back from her husband, as if surprised. "Ah, we're here. It's showtime, sweetie."

As they walked up the stairs, the door was opened and Jim bowed, then smiled at them both.

"Miss Naomi, you look wonderful!"

"Thank you, Jim. And this is my husband, William Hamilton."

Will stuck out his hand to shake the surprised Jim's hand. "Jim, is it? Ah'm pleased to meet you, sir."

Naomi's lips twitched with amusement at her husband's minor faux pas.

Jim recovered himself quickly, anxious to not make a guest feel embarrassed. "The family is in the ballroom, waiting for you to arrive. Follow me, please."

As they walked through the house, Will whispered to Naomi, "Are the *objects d'art* all around us originals?"

Naomi grinned. "Probably, but I really have no idea. They *are* one of Virginia's oldest founding families."

"Ach, Ah knew that the Scots-Irish settled around here mostly. But Ah had no idea that some of them did so well in the colonies. Ah always think of them as the hill folk with bad teeth, drinking from the still out back, playing the fiddles, and dancing barefooted in the dirt to celebrate marrying their cousins."

When Jim opened the door to the grand ballroom, Will gasped. Even Naomi was impressed since, as a child, she'd never been in much of the house beyond the foyer and Hannah's bedroom.

While they were looking all around at the opulence on display, Jim politely ushered them toward the small group of people standing near the bar.

"May I announce Mr. and Mrs. William Hamilton have arrived."

Naomi's mother stepped forward to hug each of them.

"You look beautiful, my love," she whispered to Naomi.

Her eyes lit up when she turned to Will. "And you look magnificent when you're in your full-dress regalia. I'm so pleased that my daughter was able to convince you that this is a formal occasion."

Will looked wounded. "Ah'm no a stranger to pomp and circumstance. Remember, where Ah'm from, we still have royalty."

"Even if most of them aren't popular with your countrymen, eh, Will?" Naomi's father winked at Will, and the two men shared a smile. He turned to the bar to instruct the bartender to pour a shot of single-malt Scotch into each of two glasses, then to give them a bottle of water to go with it.

"Ach, John, Ah see ye dinnae ferget how we Scotsmen enjoy our whiskey." Will nodded toward the bartender just putting his items in front of him. Will poured some of the water into his glass, then swirled it around before taking a sip. "Ah, perfect. To whom do I owe muh thanks for the *Glenlivet*?"

"That would be me." Mr. Reynolds appeared from behind John, who turned to him, aggrieved.

"But I told you what to order," he protested, claiming credit.

Henry Reynolds smiled. "Yes, so you did."

"Then Ah'm obliged to both of ye for such a treat for a Scotsman so far from his haim."

Naomi watched as the men were introduced to each other, then began discussing single-malt versus blended whiskeys. She grabbed a flute of champagne from the waiter who was just passing by them with a newly-supplied tray of filled glasses.

"Gramma!" She smiled at the approaching woman, who folded her into a huge hug.

"You look stunning, my love," Giselle murmured into her ear before releasing her. She turned to smile at the oblivious Will, who was chatting animatedly about whiskey with the host and her son-in-law. "And he looks regal. No wonder your readers are so hot to read about your Laird Duncan."

Naomi felt her face heat up in the blush. "Gramma! Stop! It's bad enough I had to listen to you and Mom extol the amenities in the honeymoon suite. Just please stop with these remarks that I don't want to hear."

Giselle turned to the grinning Marie. "Mercy! For an author of soft-core porn—excuse me, *romance novels*—your daughter's awfully touchy about treating sex like a normal bodily function that we all enjoy."

Marie's response was forgotten as their hostess approached them. Instead, she said, "Miss Elizabeth, how lovely you look tonight."

Elizabeth smiled at her, correcting her gently. "Elizabeth, remember? And thank you. You and Giselle look beautiful.

But your daughter? Naomi, dear, you look positively stunning! It appears that marriage definitely agrees with you. It's not only your face but your entire body that appears to be glowing with happiness."

Blushing again, Naomi nodded, smiling back at their hostess. She took a few steps back to reach the hand of her husband, to pull him over to introduce him. "Miss Elizabeth, may I present my husband, William Hamilton. Will, this is our hostess, Mrs. Elizabeth Reynolds."

As Elizabeth turned from speaking to Marie, she looked at Will, then gasped in surprise. Her face drained of color, and she seemed to sway on her feet. Marie was on one side of her, and Giselle moved to the other to be sure she'd have support if she fainted.

Henry Reynolds' face registered his alarm at his wife's reaction. He moved closer to her, taking her hand. "Darling, are you all right?"

Elizabeth took a deep breath to steady herself. "Of course, Henry. It's just—a bit of a shock to see a man in a kilt, who looks so much like the man from my dreams."

Naomi shot a quick glance at her husband, whose distressed look mirrored how she felt. She carefully arranged her face to reflect concern and not fear. "If I may be so bold, what dreams, Miss Elizabeth?"

"Oh, it's nothing, really. But last year, I had a dream where a man in a kilt told me that Hannah had been avenged and was now at peace." She took another deep breath before continuing. But her face was now relaxed, and her smile was genuine. "Of course I'm thrilled to meet your husband, Naomi. And I *do* know that just because he's a man in a kilt and he looks similar to the man from my dream, that doesn't mean that he's anything more than your very handsome new husband."

Will surprised Naomi by bowing and taking Elizabeth's

hand to kiss the back of it. "Ah'm honored to meet our benef-
icent hostess."

There was a pause lasting a heartbeat while everyone pro-
cessed what he had said, as well as his actions. They were
saved from the awkwardness of the moment when a waiter
appeared with a tray of canapes, and another approached
with a few flutes of champagne left on his tray.

Elizabeth smiled at her husband. "Henry, can you get me a
glass of iced tea, please?" She took Naomi's hand to lead her
over to a nearby table. "And I want to hear all about your
wedding last year. I've only seen a few pictures that you sent
to Giselle. But I'm sure there are some that show more of the
surrounding countryside. I've only been to Scotland a few
times, despite still having family there. We have about a half-
hour until the rest of our guests arrive. I want to hear all the
details, my dear."

Naomi nodded almost imperceptibly at Will as he faded
back toward the bar to continue making small talk with her
father and their host. They were soon joined by the young
men of the family, and she spent quite a while showing Miss
Elizabeth the pictures on her phone as she recounted the
magic of getting married in an arbor-altar on the grounds of
the manor owned by a friend of her husband's family.

Much later, when dinner was over and even the dessert
had been polished off, the small quartet that had been playing
quietly during dinner turned up their amps to provide dancing music. Mr. Reynolds stood to propose a toast to the happy
newlyweds, and everyone cheered, toasting to their happiness. Then he announced that the first ones on the dance floor
had to be the happy couple.

Since they'd been seated next to each other, Will stood and
offered his hand to his lady. Naomi rose up, and he led her to
the dance floor. They melted into each other's arms as if

they'd been doing it for years. They swayed gently to the slow music, and the amassed crowd clapped encouragingly.

Naomi leaned closer to her husband to whisper into his ear, "How could she have dreamed about you?"

Will met her eyes with his troubled ones. "Ah dinnae ken, lassie. Ah think the fae-folk are gone from mah heed. But they're always all around us . . . watching us . . . judging us. Who knows how they managed to intrude upon her dreams? But did ye notice she said her daughter's name aloud?"

Naomi's eyes widened. "No, I was too freaked out by what she was saying. I didn't even notice. Wow! And no one else batted an eye either, so I guess her name can be mentioned again."

She reached up to pull his face down so they could kiss. More clapping followed, and they both turned to smile at their enthusiastic audience.

"No matter," Will said softly. "She's at peace as much as her daughter's spirit is, so let's not question it."

Naomi nodded. "I'm not. I'm just quietly proud to have played a part in relieving her pain."

"Ach aye, as am mahsel'."

When the song ended, Will swept Naomi into a back-bend, then he kissed her again, to the delight of the on-lookers.

"And now, the dance floor is open. Please don't be shy — though I can't guarantee you'll enjoy it as much as our two newlyweds did."

Other couples ventured onto the dance floor, and the band changed to a more upbeat tune to encourage even more to join them. They passed an enjoyable couple of hours, dancing, resting, and snacking on the dessert bites that the waitstaff seemed to have a never-ending supply of.

Naomi pointed to her heels to plead tired feet when the dance she'd been doing with her father ended.

He nodded, then set off grinning, searching for his wife.

Naomi glanced at her watch and was surprised to see just how much time had passed. The band was good and kept the guests in a dancing mood. But when she saw Will, just being relieved of her mother as his partner by her father, she waved at him.

He smiled and strode over to her. "Can Ah finally have another dance with my lovely wife?"

Naomi grinned, pointing to her watch. "I've got a better idea, husband."

Startled, he glanced at his own watch, then his eyebrows rose. "That late already? Time flies when you're having a good time."

"Want to head back to our suite soon and have even more of a good time?" She waggled her eyebrows in an exaggerated leer and pretended to have a Cockney accent. "*Know whot Ah mean, eh?*"

"Ach aye, lassie. I'm rarin' to go another round with ye. Let me find mah jacket. Ah left it near the bar. Then we can say our goodbyes to our hosts and your family."

When Will returned, they were able to thank their host but not their hostess. They also hugged and kissed Naomi's family before making their way to the foyer.

Once out of the ballroom, Naomi stopped. "You know what? It's a bit of a drive. I think I'll go visit the powder room before we leave. Can you let Jim know we'd like the limo to take us home now?"

Will nodded, turning to find that Jim was waiting near the door and had heard them. He watched Jim head out the door to wave at their driver.

Suddenly he felt the air move around him. He turned to see Elizabeth standing in the shadows, beckoning for him to join her.

"Mrs. Reynolds? We were trying to find ye to give thanks for such a wonderful night."

"You're most welcome, Will. But I have to speak quickly before anyone notices." She peeked furtively around before leaning closer to him. "I don't know *how* you did it, or *what* you did, but I *know* you're the one who set my precious Hannah's soul free. I just want to let you know how grateful I am. When she was taken from me so suddenly, I felt like I had failed her . . . we all did. But I'm her mother, and it was my job to protect her. That's why I fell apart. I was consumed by guilt, as well as grief. Even hearing her name was like a slap, bringing all of that pain to me again."

Her expression had been that of someone suffering. Now a beatific smile lit her face. "But you freed her from the torment by getting revenge —"

When Will opened his mouth to speak, she shook her head, shushing him. "No, you don't have to tell me anything. I don't want to know. I now suspect who it was that took her from me, but that doesn't matter anymore. In letting me know she was now at peace, you freed my soul. I feel like I have my daughter back. I know she's still gone, but I can once again look at pictures of her and rejoice in the little time we did get to spend with her. And for that, I will always be grateful."

She stood on tip-toe to lightly brush each of his cheeks with a quick kiss. "You know, I grew up hearing the stories of *the little people*. I know there's strong magic in the islands. And you *are* a kinsman, since I was a Hamilton before I married. Bless you, Will Hamilton. May your days be long and happy."

Naomi strode over to them at that moment. "Miss Elizabeth, I'm so glad Will found you. We had a lovely time. Thank you so much for honoring us with such a wonderful evening. You made us feel like royalty."

Elizabeth took one of each of their hands and smiled. "I'm so happy for you. Bless you both. May your happiness continue to grow, and may your love be blessed with wee ones of your own someday."

She leaned over to deliver a quick kiss to each of Naomi's cheeks, then turned when she heard her husband's voice.

"Ah, Elizabeth, there you are. We were wondering where you had gotten to. I see you found our honored guests."

She took her husband's hand. "Yes, my love. I found them, and they've bidden their farewells." She turned to Naomi and Will. "I don't know when we'll see you again, my dears, but please don't wait for such a formal occasion. Whenever you come to visit Giselle, please stop by to let us know how you're doing."

Naomi nodded. "We will, Miss Elizabeth."

Will chimed in, "Ach aye, that we will."

Jim cleared his throat politely. "The limo is right outside the door."

Will took his wife's arm and steered her to the door. They both turned when they were at the open door and waved to their host and hostess. Then they walked down the stairs to the waiting driver and his vehicle.

Once they were in the limo, Naomi leaned toward Will with a grin. "Okay, spill it! What was she saying that was so private she pulled you into the corner? And she kissed your cheeks? Are you trying to flirt with our hostess?"

Will rolled his eyes. "No, silly woman." He looked up to check that the window between them and the driver was still closed. Satisfied, he continued. "She said she knows it really *was* me in her dreams, and she wanted to thank me for giving her back her daughter. Now that she knows Hannah's at peace, she is also."

Naomi's eyes widened. "You didn't tell her anything about *how* that happened, did you?"

Will shook his head. "Ach, Ah may look like a fool, but Ah'm nae one. And in fact, she telt me she didnae want to know how it happened. She just wanted me to know how grateful she is that her burden has been relieved."

Naomi sat back, leaning into the enveloping leather of the seat. "Hmm. I guess we'll have to hope she never shares her beliefs with anyone else, or that might lead to awkward questions."

"Remember, she said after her shock at seeing me, that she was well aware that it couldn't have been me—and that all of us Scotsmen in dress kilts look similar. Ah assume that's what she'll share with others. Ah'm reasonably certain we're safe."

Naomi leaned forward to take his hand. "And I'm positive that meeting you was good not only for her but for me. She got the closure she needed to allow her to remember her daughter with love. And I got the husband of my dreams."

Will leaned closer to cover her lips with his in a kiss that started out gentle but quickly grew in passion. When he drew back, he rested his forehead on hers as he gazed into her eyes. "And Ah got to marry the woman Ah've wanted since the first time Ah saw ye. And we've begun creating our own *happily-ever-after*."

Naomi's lips curved up in a smile. "I've written so many *HEA's* for my characters. It's a joy to have one for myself in real life. And it's all thanks to your Gaelic magic, my laird."

They resumed making out, steaming up all of the windows before the limo stopped. Then they made their way up to their hotel room to continue the romance that was so much better than anything even Naomi had ever written.

The End

ABOUT THE AUTHOR

Mom taught me to read when I was five. Since then, I have always had characters intruding into my thoughts, showing scenes from their lives. When I ignore them, they start to yell louder. If I write their stories so they can live in readers' heads as well, they usually leave me alone . . .until the next voices appear. I like the noise.

Learn more about me and my books, read excerpts and reviews, at: www.fionamcgier.com

Or come visit me on Facebook:

https://www.facebook.com/fiona.mcgier/

www.ingramcontent.com/pod-product-compliance
Lightning Source LLC
Chambersburg PA
CBHW060825120626
46557CB00001B/369